Throwdown
© Dale Hoagland, 2019

Printed in The United States of America

A few decades ago, when law enforcement officers hit the street, they sometimes carried a "throw down." It served two functions. If your duty weapon jammed or was lost in a fight, you'd have a second weapon. And if you accidentally killed an unarmed man, you could throw down the unregistered gun to cover your mistake.

THROWDOWN

THE INVISIBLE RULES

By Dale Hoagland

CHAPTER 1

The human animal struggles to balance adventure and security. It's an arc that makes children want the safety of their mothers, teens freedom from supervision, young adults adventure, and the aged a love of their recliner and bed. Policework relies on the middle stage of life. Young adults who can handle the violence, danger and insecurity inherent in the profession. It also relies on the judgement of older cops to control the adventuresome.

That's why Lieutenant Bud Glen and all the other administrators at San Jose PD were constantly fine tuning the next generation of leaders. The problem was that this new generation had a different view of the world, and making it all work required compromise on both sides.

Administration didn't like promoting Sergeants without sending them to patrol. It was standard practice in all law enforcement agencies to send newly promoted Sergeants to patrol to get the experience they needed to understand the basic supervision function in policing. Patrol was where it all happened. It wasn't sexy or creative like detective work or special assignments, but it was where all real police work started and it was where all Sergeants needed to start.

Administrators also had one other consideration when they rotated officers back to patrol from special assignments. It stopped them from being corrupted by the streets. The theory was that a lot of narcs were ruined by their freewheeling street life and needed a reintroduction to "normal life and normal people." The quote Chiefs and Sheriffs used relentlessly was, "Once you've laid down with dogs you never get rid of the fleas."

That's why the administration wanted the new narc/gang Sergeants to be assigned to patrol duties. They were wild and out of control and needed adult supervision. The problem was the narc squad didn't have any replacement for the two new Sergeants, Cameron Michaelson and Erin Fulham. When they were promoted to Sergeant, they were left in place at the squad. They had recently been part of a major bust that made arrests in three cities and identified a DEA agent gone bad. Their creative tactics stopped large amounts of fentanyl from reaching the streets and shut down a serious organized crime operation. Embarrassingly, they also discovered some unprofessional conduct at the highest levels of the police department. Sometimes police administrators valued discretion over integrity. In other words, the narcs embarrassed the police administration.

Captain Johnson, who was supervisor of the Investigation Division, told the Chief, "Fine, you can rotate them to patrol. Who've you got to replace them? Cause I need someone that knows how to manage narcs, gang investigations and all the other assorted crazy shit that lands in their unit. You may not like the situation, but it not a matter of what we like. It's a matter of what we have to work with."

The Chief was pissed. He didn't like it when his Captains didn't agree with him. If he were staffed like he was supposed to be, he wouldn't have these problems, so he did what any good administrator did in situations like these: he threw it back on his subordinates to find an answer.

"Okay, Captain, you know the problem. Come up with a solution. Dismissed."

Johnson left the Chief's office with a cool calm smile on his face. Inside he was thinking, "What a horse's ass. He doesn't have a fricking idea how to fix this, so I have to do his job for him." It was crap like this that gave Captains stress-induced heart attacks.

Johnson called in Lieutenant Glen who was just back from a sailing vacation with his girlfriend.

"Bud, we have a problem."

Glen eased his 6-foot 5-inch, 250 lb. frame into a chair in front of the Captain's desk and waited, thinking, "Welcome back Bud. Here we go again. A classic case of vacation whiplash."

"The Chief thinks we need to transfer Cam and Erin into patrol for their normal promotion rotation. He's getting heat from someone, probably the city council. I told him that we don't have anyone qualified to replace them and that they've displayed exemplary judgement repeatedly in a highly volatile job. He was unmoved and told me to find a solution."

"Interesting," Lieutenant Glen said. "His problem and you're to find a solution. What would happen if you told him you came up dry and threw the ball back in his court?"

Johnson ran his hand through what sparse traces of hair remained on his head and said, "I hate to imagine what he would dream up."

Glen stood up and said, "I'll chat with the gang and see what we can come up with." Glen walked toward the door. What Glen also knew was that the Chief and his political allies thought Cam and his fellow narcs needed neutering. Their wild tactics were troubling to the straight laced, not to mention the fact that outing the corrupt DEA agent showed some sleazy ethics a little closer to home.

"Bud, don't even think of retiring. I'm an old man with a weak heart and you could be responsible for my death."

Bud smiled, "Nice try, Captain. Guilt hasn't worked on me since my mom tried it when I was ten."

Bud didn't always work so agreeably with Captain Johnson. Johnson had investigated Glen in the past for a use of force case where Glen killed a crook with a neck restraint hold. The Captain and Glen became more trusting of one another over the years, Glen suspected because time had mellowed them both.

∞

Cam and Bobby were trying to put together a raid on a biker house that was dealing every drug imaginable. The crooks sold to an informant that was reliable by court standards, so a search warrant had been drafted by the narc supervising the informant, Tommy Aquilar. Tommy debriefed the informant and the more he heard, the more concerned he got about the safety of this warrant service. These crooks all serve joint time and were armed to the teeth with serious weapons. They also had two dogs chained to the front and back porch area. Cops weren't getting in those doors without neutralizing those dogs. That would cause a huge delay that was dangerous.

The fourth amendment of the Constitution required you to "knock and notice" the occupants. In other words, tell them who you were and the purpose of your visit. You had to demand admittance and allow the occupants "reasonable" time to respond. The exception to this was when it was deemed too dangerous or evidence was being destroyed; then you could force entry. Sometimes cops made that decision in seconds.

As Cam was reviewing the details of this house with Tommy, Bobby said, "I had to shoot a dog on a meth raid last year and I don't want to do that again." Bobby being a gentle soul wasn't sure whether his old partner Cam understood his passive side. Cam could be a little harsh sometimes.

Cam thought a few seconds and said, "Bobby, call animal control and see if they've got any tricks that would work on these pooches."

Then he turned to his Corporal, Jesse Hale. "Jesse, how 'bout you come up with a way to get in that house without a full-blown gun battle?"

Never too deferential to authority, Jesse, a big Hawaiian, said, "Sure, Sergeant, just give me a minute to pull something great out of my butt."

Cam smiled at Jesse, "Can't wait to see what you pop out."

Jesse was famous on the squad for his creativity. He and Randy Keen had gotten into a major dealer's fortified house that had a thick metal bar across the door by cutting the door hinges and making the door swing around the metal security bar like a pet door. After that, Jesse and Randy were the go-to guys for all problems in need of a genius.

Cam told everybody to have some ideas ready for the day after tomorrow because the dope was going to arrive at the dealer's about 2:00 pm and he wanted to hit the house by 4:00 pm.

∞

Cam arrived home that evening to the most terrifying news he'd ever received in his life. He and his wife Jane had been trying to have a kid for about six months and had also agreed to adopt an 18-month-old baby that belonged to a shirt-tail relative of Jane's. The baby's mother had been killed in an auto accident and the father wasn't in the picture anymore. The grandmother that was raising the child recognized that she was too old to give the child the parenting her daughter would have wanted for the baby. Cam and Jane were the answer to a prayer for her and it would allow her to move back into the grandmother role she really wanted. They were scheduled to sign the paperwork later that month and had been taking the baby for extended stays to get everyone adjusted to the change. Jane was already in love with the baby and Cam knew it was a done deal. There was no backing out now.

As he entered the house, he knew something was up because not only did his German Shepard Nick greet him with his usual tail wags and insistence on a head rub, but Jane was there with a beer and a couple of steaks marinating for the BBQ.

She looked nervous and he knew she was wanting to share something, so he said, "Okay, why don't we go sit on the porch so you can tell me a story."

Jane smiled, "It's a good one."

Cam sat down, kicked off his shoes and took a sip of his cold beer. He waited.

"Well, you know I love this kid we're adopting, right?"

Cam replied, "Ya, right."

"Well, I went to the doctor, you know, about the pregnancy thing."

"Yes?"

"I'm pregnant."

Cam's eyes dilated, "Any idea who the father is?"

Jane was holding Nick's hair brush and threw it at Cam, bouncing it off his shoulder.

"Jerk."

Cam laughed, "What are you mad about? I'm the one that went from single to a family of four?"

Jane stood up, announcing as she went into the kitchen, "Actually five. We're having twins."

Cam just sat for a while, then he went into the kitchen and said, "For real? Cause this would really be a bad joke."

"For real, but look at the bright side, I won't be bugging you for more kids."

Cam gave her a big hug and kiss. He held her by the arms at his arm's length, "Holy shit!"

She smiled back at him, "Kind of leaves your head spinning, doesn't it?"

"Yes, I've got a million questions, but I guess those will wait. How are you with all this?

"Scared, excited, worried, and so happy I could dance."

In the back of Cam's consciousness, he registered that his responsibilities in life had just increased exponentially.

CHAPTER 2

Corporal Jesse Hale had worked up a raid plan with Randy's help and it was one for the books. Cam had all personnel assigned to the search warrant service assemble in the training room for a briefing.

"Okay, everybody listen up. The king of Kona has a plan for hitting this house and timing is critical, so we need your full attention. Jesse."

"All right guys, according to the informant this place is full of ex-cons and bikers and we need to get the crooks outside or at least to open the door without them knowing they're about to get raided. Their house sits on a corner lot and that allows us to stage an auto accident right in front of the home. It apparently happens a lot there anyway, because one street has a yield sign where people don't yield. Randy talked with an auto wrecker that hauls a lot of our cars and he's got two wrecks that will work. The plan is to set one that's not drivable in motion by pushing it with another truck and for the drivable vehicle to T-bone it up onto the crook's front lawn.

That ought to get them out of the house. We'll have groups of officers in several locations that will rush the place when the crooks come out to see the wreck.

"I've worked up an assignment sheet with everybody's placement I'll hand out."

Cam stepped up beside Jesse while everyone was reading the assignment sheet, "Questions?"

Erin asked, "Who's driving the crash car?"

Jesse looked at Randy, so he stood up and said, "The wrecking yard owner's teenage son. He does demolition derbies every year at the county fair, so this is second nature for him."

Todd stuck his hand up, signaling a question, "Cam, about the dogs?"

Cam looked at Bobby, "Yeah'" said Bobby, "The dogs. Well, the animal control guys said they'd send a couple of people over to help. I guess their tactic is to use a road flare shoved in the dog's face. Dogs are afraid of fire so they back off pretty quick. They'll also have one of those dog loops that slips over the dog's neck on a stiff pole if the flare doesn't do it."

Cam and Jesse fielded a few more questions and Cam went over specific assignments during the raid. Tommy was in charge of the paperwork and recovery of all the property for report purposes. They couldn't have fifteen cops all finding property and all of them being subpoenaed to court, so the officers would locate the evidence to be seized, then have Tommy secure it for the chain of custody. As with all search warrant services, the entry into the house was the dangerous part. Once you were inside and the crooks were secured everything was under control, but the element of surprise was critical. If someone saw you coming and warned the occupants things turned deadly quickly.

The narc squad had an assortment of magnetic signs they could slap on any vehicle to make it look like it belonged in the neighborhood. The one they used for the biker house was a yard maintenance business, "Garcia Lawn Care." They even had a small trailer with mowers and tools attached to the back of the van that they borrowed from the city public works department. The van was full of cops that would rush out the sliding side door when the crook's front door was open.

There were two rear doors that needed to be covered, so Jesse had two officers each assigned to cover those when the signal went out. Both of those two officer teams arrived in different cars a half block away and walked back to the general area of the house. The rear units weren't necessarily supposed to make entry unless it was easy. Their job was to stop suspects from escaping out the back with the dope. When everybody was in their pre-raid staging area it became Cam's job to direct the proper sequence of moves. The auto wrecker cars were in position a half block away and both of their drivers had police radios, so they could be told when to start their run.

Cam keyed his mic, "Jesse, get the van in position," which was right next door to the target house. "Todd, Erin, park and walk." They were covering the two rear doors. When Cam saw the van pull up, he radioed the auto wrecker drivers, "John and Austin, start your run."

John was driving a pickup truck with push bars that they used to move wrecks around the wrecker's yard. It wasn't licensed for the street but somehow, he didn't think he'd be getting a ticket today. John started to push the junk vehicle with a strapped down steering wheel forward at a very slow speed, as Austin calculated speed and distance to get the impact dead center of the vehicle and with sufficient force to roll it up on the front lawn of the crook's house.

Randy was concerned when he worked out this scheme with these two guys, that this would work properly. They assured him that they had plenty of experience staging accidents for school safety programs and demolition derbies. They were right. John got the junk car moving slowly, then jammed on the truck's brakes to set it free. He then cranked the steering wheel and sped off down the street away from the house. Austin hit the driverless car dead center on his projected mark and the car made a huge crashing sound as it rolled on its side. The lack of an engine or transmission made it light and easy to roll. Austin's car was reinforced to take a head-on impact even though the crash was a low-speed hit and Austin followed Randy's instructions and backed up out of the area so he wouldn't be in danger of being in the middle of a gun battle. John and Austin couldn't help themselves, and found an observation spot for a good view of the raid.

The plan worked perfectly. Six half-loaded bikers came out the front door and circled around the car laying on its side on their lawn to see what happened. They couldn't figure out where the driver was, but started to understand what was happening when eight officers exited the lawn care van. Cam ran across the street to the house and met with two SWAT officers, a Parole Agent and a pound officer who followed him while Tommy and three other officers took down the bikers at the wrecked car.

Cam announced, "Police Officer, Search Warrant" as he entered the open door and the officers spread out through the house looking for other occupants. The pound guy had the dog backed up to the end of his chain barking and whining.

While all this getting ready to go down, Todd, Al and another pound employee were hidden near the rear door attempting to be quiet before the crash occurred. Just when they thought all was well the rear door opened and a fat, middle-aged biker walked out with a box full of computer components. He was barefoot and Todd was fairly sure unarmed because he had on a pair of pants and no shirt. He walked toward a parked Cadillac and popped the trunk. The problem Todd was faced with was that if the crook turned around, he'd see Todd and might warn the others. So, Todd ran up behind the guy and said, "Police, down on your knees." Todd slammed his left foot behind the guy's left knee, dropping him to his knees instantly. The crook dropped his cardboard box and Todd grabbed both his hands and cuffed them behind his back.

Before the crook could figure out what was happening Todd said, "Stand up." As soon as he was standing Todd grabbed a handful of his hair with his left hand and forced his head down level with his waist. With his right hand he grabbed the back of his pants and threw him in the trunk, slamming the lid. Todd always had to remember to pull his punches when he handled people. He was a serious weight lifter and was so strong he could hurt suspects accidentally.

"Now," Todd said, "The raid can go down."

Al shook his head, "Just when I think you don't have any more surprises you prove me wrong."

Todd and Al arrived at the back door as Cam was yelling, "Police Officer Search Warrant." That meant they were clear to enter. The dog wasn't barking, but was growling and it left little doubt about its willingness to bite the cops. The pound guy slipped a pole leash over the dog's head and pulled it away from the door, so Todd and Al could go in. The crook had left the back door open when he stepped out, so Todd opened the door all the way. Stepping inside he announced, "Police Officer, Search Warrant," primarily so the crooks and the cops coming in from the front knew who he was.

The door Erin was posted at looked to be unused as there was a pile of boxes and furniture in front of it, so she and the reserve officer she had assigned to her went in behind Todd and Al.

As all the officers spread out inside the house, they met little resistance. The SWAT officers all used shotguns because it was the ideal weapon for close quarters defense. It was lethal at a range of ten to twenty feet and didn't risk hitting people in adjacent rooms.

As Cam and the Parole Officer came to the back-master bedroom, Cam thought he heard a noise inside, so he did a tactical entry into the room by grabbing the door casing with his left hand and extending his Glock 40 cal. through the door aimed at the king-sized bed. With just a small portion of his head visible, he saw the biker who owned the house sitting up in his bed with one foot on the floor reaching down for a rifle laying on the carpet. His head was lowered, so he didn't see Cam even though he had to have heard the officers yelling their announcement as they proceeded through the house. The crook and his girlfriend were both naked in bed with only a sheet covering them. Apparently, they were having a little afternoon recreation when the cops arrived. Cam knew from the briefing material that this crook was a violent and dangerous threat, so he said nothing because that would only distract him. He locked his sight picture on the crook's head and started to remove all the trigger slack as the crook reached for the gun. Cam's weapon was on target and he was a fraction of a second from executing a triple tap into the crook's head when his naked girlfriend looked at Cam and realized that this cop wasn't saying a word and was waiting till her boyfriend touched the gun. She screamed which caused the crook to look up and see Cam with one eye squinted and a gun zeroed in on his head.

He raised his hands and said, "I surrender. Don't shoot man."

Cam said, "Hands high and face the wall. You too sweetheart."

Both the bed occupants walked forward on either side of the bed and placed their hands on the wall. The parole officer cuffed them both then jerked the sheet off the bed and threw it around the shoulders of the woman.

The Parole Officer, Danny Dominquez, told Cam, "He's one of mine. I'm surprised he didn't go for the gun. He's a psychopath. I'll put a parole hold on him so he won't get to bail, but I'm not sure how long I can keep him if you don't have decent charges to hit him with."

After the house was secured, all the crooks cuffed and under watch in the living room, Cam started a conversation with Danny. "Why can't you guys hold this asshole longer?"

"The determinate sentencing laws give an exact sentence now, except for a select few offenses. The old days of five to life are no more, so once a guy's done his time the parole window is short. After that he's a free man. This is an example of why the five to life was a better sentence. A parole board would never have turned him loose. He's ganged up, violent and its a given he'll offend again soon. We get a lot of guys like this. We know they'll screw up, you just hope they don't hurt too many people in the process. The ex-con with a firearm should get him a little time."

Cam's brain was processing more information than he could handle right then, but he said, "Danny, what's your case load consist of right now?"

"I've got about thirty-five high-risk offenders. Mostly violent crime offenders and gang members. Another guy in my office has a few, but most of his load are sex offenders. All my guys are deemed likely to re-offend and 90% of them do eventually."

Cam was busy right now but he needed to get all the information he could from this guy. He was a valuable resource. "Danny, any way I can get a list of these guys and talk with you about them?"

"Sure, call me at the office sometime and I'll get you all the poop you want. There is an on-line link for law enforcement, but you'll get better local information if you and I sit down and talk."

"Great. I'll call you." Cam shook hands with him and went to see how his troops were, processing all the prisoners and seized evidence.

Erin had everything coordinated efficiently as usual, and Tommy was getting help on his end from the evidence techs. As they stood around Erin was asking about radio counts to make sure the portables were all accounted for and everything was secured.

"Erin announced to Cam, "I called for prisoner transport, so we should be out of here shortly."

Al looked at Todd, "Hey, Big Guy, did you let that dude out of the trunk yet?"

Todd gritted his teeth and said, "Oh shit!" as he ran to the back of the house.

CHAPTER 3

Cam was an early riser. He tried to sleep in on his days off, but this Saturday was like every other day to his internal clock, so he awakened at 5:30 a.m. Jane joined him an hour later on the front deck for coffee and a look at the paper.

"Well Mom, what's the day look like for you?"

"Aren't you sweet. I'm going to yoga with Erin and then some shopping. I've got big plans for the bedrooms around here."

"Swell, do I get a say in the remodel?"

"About the baby rooms? No."

Cam laughed, "Sorry, dumb question. I think Nick and I will go for a run." He stood up kissed her and put on his running clothes.

"Hey, is Erin coming back here with you?"

"I think so, we're looking at colors for the rooms."

He nodded, "Love you. Come on, Nick."

∞

When Jane and Erin returned the three of them sat down for lunch. Erin couldn't help laughing at Cam's changed life. As Jane got up to clear the table Erin said, "Boy, has your world done a 180."

"Enjoying this, aren't you?"

"Immensely!"

"Hey, have you given any thought to the problem Lieutenant Glen laid on us the other day?"

Erin nodded, "I have. The administration isn't going to let this go. They want all new Sergeants to have patrol experience, so I thought we might compromise a little, which would allow them to save face and meet the technical requirements they want, and not really cause us that much grief."

Cam said, "I'm listening."

"Each of us does one shift a week on patrol on either a Friday or Saturday night. That way patrol will have some supervisor coverage and we'll get patrol experience and Glen gets to keep his supervisors without a major disruption."

Cam thought about it for a few seconds, "That's not bad and if anybody could sell it, it would be Lieutenant Glen. It might even be fun to get patrol involved in some of our investigations. They're a large manpower source."

Erin smiled, "Leave it to you to think of patrol as uniformed narcs. After six months of us running a weekend patrol shift the brass will be glad to get rid of us."

∞

Lieutenant Glen read the proposal that Erin drafted and said, to no one in particular, "Could work." He really believed this whole push was more an effort to neutralize the threat that the narcs posed to a controlled environment. For people who lived in a political world, their creativity could be unsettling.

The Captain made Glen come to a meeting with the Chief to pitch this unique idea because he knew the Chief was intimidated by Glen. There was chain of command authority and there was physical authority. Glen was not only a large man at 6 foot 5 and 250 pounds, but he gave anybody talking with him the impression that he could snap their spine for little cause. The fact that he'd been a Special Forces Navy diver and an African mercenary sent people's imagination into overdrive. Then there was the incident where he accidental broke a crook's neck. Even veteran cops weren't completely sure they were safe.

∞

The old uniform with new stripes felt both strange and familiar all at once to Cam. This whole thing would take some getting used to.

Glen had asked them, "Who wants Friday and who wants Saturday?"

Erin said, "Give me Friday so I can have Saturday date night free. Cam doesn't need Saturday's off. He won't be going on a date for at least fifteen years."

Glen wasn't sure what the joke was and Cam walked away thinking, "She's probably right."

∞

Terrence was between trainees when Cam started his Saturday evening patrol shift, so he crawled into Cam's supervisor unit to ride with him a while.

"Okay, white boy, I trained your old partner Bobby, so I guess I can train you to be a Sergeant."

"I can use all the help I can get, Terrence." And Cam meant it. He knew how to supervise cops, but patrol was a different animal and he'd been away for a few years. Most of the stuff he needed help with was procedural and Terrence knew all the rules.

Cam was amazed that there was no training procedure for Sergeants, but after a couple of nights where Terrence shadowed him for several hours a shift Terrence announced, "Okay you got this, there's a point where every artist is just scratching the canvas."

"Terrence, I owe you."

Terrence smiled and gave Cam the queen's wave, arm held high and a limp wrist circle.

Erin got a similar assist from her old boyfriend from five years ago. They were still friends and he was working the preceding shift, so he just hung around a few hours of her watch and helped. She also had several other officers on her watch that knew her and answered any questions she had. She actually liked patrol for a change. Not that she wanted it over the narc squad, but there was something about the patrol assignment what was controlled and predictable. Mostly, it ended at the end of your watch, unlike special assignments.

CHAPTER 4

At about 10:00 pm Erin overheard dispatch assign a suspected rape to one of her male officers, Robert Volk. She had dispatch send a female officer to assist because it always helped to have female cops present when female rape victims were involved. The female officer, Anna Sims, was an LAPD transplant and had excellent experience when she took a lateral transfer to SJPD. Anna would eventually call the rape crisis center to get long-term support for the victim, but wanted to do the interview first to see where this was going before injecting other people that might get in the way. The male cop assigned was glad for the help, so he started a report while Anna asked the questions.

The victim was a 23-year-old college student who had been drinking at a local bar patronized by college aged people. Gwen Abbott was smart, and articulate in her description of events. The problem was, the rape had occurred the evening prior to this.

As all three of them sat around Gwen's kitchen table, Anna asked, "Okay, Gwen, why the delay in reporting this?"

"I was drugged and I just now got my head clear enough to figure it all out. I drove home and went to bed because I was so screwed up. I woke up about two hours ago and called after I started to think about all this."

Officer Bob Volk asked a couple of report questions. "Do you know the suspect?"

"No."

"Any description?"

"No."

Where did all this occur?"

"A bar called The Dorm."

Anna said, "Ya, we're familiar with the place."

As the story began to unfold Gwen explained that she had gone there to meet some girlfriends and had chatted with some guys and girls she knew, but her friends never arrived. She said she had about three drinks, had a couple of dances and was a little drunk, but not passing out drunk. The next thing she knew she was waking up in her car in the bar parking lot at 10:00 am. and everything was wrong.

Anna said, "Explain, everything was wrong?"

Gwen answered while counting on her fingers, "My car was parked against a rear fence about as far from the bar entrance as you can get. I never would have parked there. It's not safe. When I took off my bra at home, I noticed it was the wrong hook. I always set it on the tightest setting. My underwear was damp, and my thighs and hips were sore like I'd had sex. Not gentle sex, and I don't remember a thing. Even some of the bar memories are gone. I'm sure someone drugged me and raped me."

Bob wanted to ask about the possibility she was drunk and had just gone to the car with someone voluntarily, but figured Anna would get around to that and it would look bad if he asked it.

Sure enough, Anna said, "Gwen, rape is rape and if you didn't give consent, you were raped, but is there any possibility you went to the car with an old boyfriend or someone you just met?"

"No. I don't believe that."

Officer Volk said, "Okay, Gwen, here's the deal. We're going to transport you to the hospital for a rape kit and exam. Anna will explain how all that works."

Gwen said, "Can I drive myself? I've got things to do today."

Anna answered, "We need to have ID come out and run some tests inside your car. It's possible there may be some DNA evidence or prints. Bob will stay here for that and I'll run you over to the hospital. We'll need the clothes you were wearing that night. Judging from your wet hair, I assume you've showered?"

"Yes, I guess that wasn't too smart."

Anna nodded, "That's okay, we might still get something."

The medical exam results weren't all that helpful. Whoever assaulted Gwen Abbott used a condom. There was evidence of a lubricated condom. All of this confirmed a sexual assault because the victim hadn't had any exposure to either condoms or lubricant for some time. Because Anna had been involved with "roofies" as a Los Angeles officer she knew that a blood test was not likely to show much. Rohypnol and most other date rape drugs leave the body too soon. Ketamine would still show up in the blood, but Anna was betting on rohypnol because of the symptoms. That's why she asked for a urine test. It will show the drug up to three days.

The forensic work on the car found nothing useful. The techs noted in the report that the car looked to have been wiped down because even Gwen's prints were missing.

Erin called in Bob and Anna the following Friday when she was pulling her patrol shift.

"Alright guys, what have you got to tell me about this rape?"

Anna started, "We handed it off to sexual assault investigative unit detectives, but as far as I can tell, she was raped. The drug scan isn't final but looks like roofies, which is weird because there are easier drugs to get these days. They haven't been prescribed for years."

Bob added, "They're legal in over 60 countries, so they're still out there. One of the byproducts of the Bill Cosby trial was that everyone knows how easy it is to rape someone with drugs."

Erin said, "Yep, a free press warns the innocent and trains the guilty. Bob, I'd like you to hit that bar and a few other college age bars and see if they have any similar cases. Maybe if you pull a photo of our victim you can get someone who remembers her and saw something."

Bob, who didn't look for extra work, asked, "So, we're detectives now?" On some level Bob knew that this was not how patrol did things and this new narc Sergeant was rewriting the rules.

Erin wasn't accustomed to push-back from officers. The narcs and gang officers respected her and seldom complained when she asked them to do something.

"Officer Volk, I'd like you to investigate this like it was your daughter who was raped last week. You know as well as I do that detectives are really busy right now and this could be an ongoing crime. Time matters here and I've looked at your work stats. You're not that busy."

Duly chastised, Bob said, "No problem, I'm on it."

Erin looked at Anna. "Anna, do a computer scan for any reports that could match this incident, suspicious persons, assaults, bouncers throwing out customers, you know?"

"Will do, Sarge."

CHAPTER 5

Cam was frequently amazed that the criminal justice system turned loose people they had designated as "high risk." If they knew they were dangerous and likely to reoffend, why would you take a chance? He wondered if he could start a "go fund me" project to buy houses next to judges, so he could rent them to parolees. If they had to live next door to these guys maybe they'd be more careful who they let out.

He sat down with Danny Dominquez in the parole office and went over a list of potential repeat offenders. Danny had printed out the hot sheet, then Cam made notes on the side and attached supporting material that Danny provided him.

"Danny, there's a lot of bad dudes here."

"Yep, and there's more on the way. A bunch of gang members were sent up on a minor third strike, so some folks got it in their head that giving them a break was a good idea. The fact is, DAs all over the state used that third strike to take some real nasty assholes out of circulation, but it looks like we're getting a bunch back. They'll screw up again, and the cost to the public will likely be serious."

"I need to run these rap sheets and gang profiles through a computer program and see what it predicts. I'm guessing we might be able to stop some of these guys before they hurt too many folks."

Danny smiled at Cam and said, "Well, I'm not sure what you have in mind, but your reputation precedes you, so I'm happy to help." Cam's image across law enforcement was legendary and was often exaggerated on the retelling of each story.

Cam shook his hand, grabbed a pile of paperwork and headed back to the office. He had to think this thing over. "Am I doing patrol work or narcs/gang work?" He guessed it really didn't matter because it was all police work.

∞

It was a Tuesday, which meant Sergeants Cam and Erin, got together with Corporals Bobby and Jesse for an informal narc staff meeting. The idea was to discuss cases they were working on and how to cross reference information and labor.

Erin started by explaining her rohypnol case. "I'm not completely sure who should control this investigation. Narcs handle dope, detectives handle rape and patrol can get involved in any in-progress crime."

Jesse, who happened to be dating Erin, added. "Well, wherever it finds a home, I'd contact the sex crimes dicks. I worked over there for a year and they've got a pretty good data bank on local perverts. They also use a lot of on-line integrated programs to link things."

Erin nodded and made a few notes. She looked at Cam and said, "My patrol people are kind of whiney when I make them do investigation work, so maybe getting sex crimes to deal with it makes sense."

Cam nodded, "If we can get a lead on the rohypnol, we can run with it."

Cam brought up the biker raid and complimented Jesse on the distraction wreck that got them into the house so easily. "You know, Big Kahuna, you keep setting yourself up as the genius tactician that can solve all problems."

Jesse smiled, "Swell, no pressure there."

Cam explained about his arrest of the biker house owner at gun point and how it was extremely close to a shooting incident. He explained the conversation with Danny Dominguez the parole officer and the data he'd gotten from him. "There has to be a way we can use this to anticipate some crimes."

Everyone was quiet for a few seconds, trying to come up with some practical ideas, when Bobby spoke up.

"There's no reason to reinvent the wheel here. It's been done before.

Erin said, "Okay professor, elaborate and elucidate."

Bobby grinned at her. "Years ago, LAPD had a stake out detail that tracked recently paroled crooks that were predicted to reoffend and go back to prison. The parole officer liaisoned with the PD and they gave them a list of the most dangerous ones. They would follow them and catch them casing banks and stores to rob, then the team would set up on the businesses when it was about to go down. The result was almost always dead crooks because these dudes were violent and just out of prison, so they didn't want to go back. The PD got a lot of heat because they didn't arrest the crooks before the robbery and the citizens felt like they were being used like bait. The cops knew it was hard to prove attempted robbery. Public pressure forced them to shut down the squad."

"The other example of high-tech that comes to mind is the Lazar Program. Some law enforcement agencies, including LA, bought it on a grant. It was made by the CIA for predicting crime. You dump a lot of data in and it spits some predictions out."

Cam said, "I don't see the department going for the money to chase down a long shot like this, but there's no reason we couldn't do a combination low and high-tech version of this. There have to be programs we could use to help us with guesstimates, right?"

Jesse nodded, "I don't see why not. Who are our resident computer experts beside Bobby?"

Bobby said, "Paul is good but he's gone native, south of the border."

Cam added, "Right, that Teresa thing." Paul had worked with an informant on the fentanyl case and allowed her to live with him. Things evolved and he went to live with her in Central America. "What about his buddy, Data? Al Sylvester has some contact information on him, although I really think this plan is more about good old-fashioned police work and stakeouts."

Bobby said, "I'll talk with Al and see what Data thinks. You need to tutor me on the list of baddies parole gave you."

Cam nodded. "Okay guys, rock and roll."

As everyone got up to leave Cam said, "Erin, a minute."

When they were alone Cam said, "I've got a patrol problem that needs a female perspective."

Erin sarcastically said, "Aren't all your pending family members female? I thought you were an expert on women."

Cam said, "Ya, I'm a real pro, that's why I got into this mess. I've been put in charge of the FTO program (field training officer) and all my trainers are telling me I've got a problem female trainee that needs to be failed. She's going to raise a shit storm and everybody is walking on eggs. In the current political environment, it's dangerous to fire females. On top of that, administration thinks any woman will satisfy their critics and they're caving every time we have one of these problems."

Erin asked, "Are you sure they gave her a fair shake? You guys can be real jerks to women sometimes."

"I'm thinking, yes. These are good trainers."

"Cam, how long did it take you to trust me as a fellow cop? How many months before you said, She's okay? She'll be there when I need her."

"I don't know, a few months I guess."

"Maybe a year?"

Cam answered, "Ya, okay. Maybe a year."

"And how long did it take for you to trust Bobby?"

"Okay, Erin, I get it. Women have a hard time getting acceptance in police work, but you know as well as I do that some people aren't cut out for this."

She nodded and said, "Anna Sims is an FTO. Schedule your problem for training with Anna. If she needs to be bounced, she'll know and you won't take as much heat if it comes from a woman."

Cam said, "Thanks Erin, that's a great idea." As he walked away, he thought, "Why do I surround myself with all these ball busting women?"

CHAPTER 6

Randy had yet another great idea, now all he had to do was get some supervisor to buy into it. He did a little head scratching and tried to Ouija board an answer. His solution was to start small with Corporal Hale.

"Jesse, you got a minute?"

Jesse squinted his eyes over his cup of black coffee. "Randolph Keen - before caffeine - is just plan mean."

"Funny, but I really need to talk with you because I got this great idea."

Jesse invited him into the Corporal's office and pulled up a chair for him beside his desk. Jesse kicked off his shoes because years as a barefoot boy in Hawaii had made him hate wearing shoes.

"Okay, Randy, lay it on me."

"Okay, stay with me on this one. It's slightly complicated. Cam and Erin working with patrol gave me an idea for a joint operation. You know how the courts have ruled it's lawful to have sobriety check points even though you don't really have any probable cause to believe a crime has been committed because there's a compelling public interest and the intrusion on people's 4th amendment right is minimal?"

"Ya...."

"How about we bring in a dope dog and a gun powder dog to sniff the car while we're asking about alcohol and handing out our safety pamphlets?"

"I don't know Randy, the courts might view the extension into other areas as illegal."

"They might, but they've already ruled that pretext stops are okay. You can stop a drug transport vehicle for a traffic violation even though you really want a dog to sniff for dope. They've ruled on it repeatedly. So, our dog search would be a logical extension of the pretext stop. We stop them legally for a sobriety check, or have them drive through a check point, then we really don't delay them. The traffic cop checks for alcohol use while the dog walks around the car. If the dog alerts, we have probable cause for a search. We could catch a lot of gang bangers with dope and guns. Some agencies are already doing this."

Jesse leaned back in his chair and put his shoeless feet on a short file cabinet next to his desk. "Your logic is convincing, but getting Cam or Erin to bite will be another trick."

Randy knew Jesse was seeing Erin, so he had to tread lightly, "I recommend Cam, Erin thinks I'm loony tunes anyway."

Jesse stood up and said, "We all do Randy, but okay, I'll lay it on Cam."

"Thanks Jesse."

∞

Cam, Jesse and Al were running loose surveillance on an informant's covered buy. He told Al that he had two sources of heroin he was willing to give up for help with a burglary charge he had pending. Which of course, meant they weren't his best connection because he still needed to buy a fix twice a day and didn't want to lose his best connection. Al told him that if he did the covered buys and the search warrants were successful, he would recommend probation on the burglary. The informant was supplied with money and the officers followed him to two different homes. He was searched before he went in to assure he didn't have any drugs on him or in his car. They watched him enter the house and followed him to a park where he turned over heroin to the narcs. They could therefore state in the warrant affidavit, he bought it at the house they were watching. Al thought the informant might have pinched some of the purchase out of the $50 bag because his pupils looked constricted, but he couldn't prove it. He'd called him on it, but the guy denied it. Junkies lie almost as much as politicians.

As Cam and Jesse sat in their undercover car and watched Al deal with his informant, Jesse ran down Randy's idea to Cam.

"You know, Jesse, as crazy as it all sounds it's not a bad idea. I have no doubt the courts will be difficult to convince, but our job isn't to anticipate court rejection. We should be presenting new options for enforcement and hope for approval. There are a bunch of case decisions that are a result of cops trying new things."

Jesse said, "You're as crazy as he is." They both laughed. "The problem with all this, Cam, is that the DA's Office won't sanction it because it's different and our administrators are so lawsuit adverse, that they won't go for it either."

"True, but who said anything about asking them? How does that saying go, it's always easier to ask for forgiveness than permission?"

"You know, Cam, some people thought you becoming a family man would make you more cautious. I see no evidence of that at all."

Cam laughed, "Work with the gang and set up a tentative date to do this. We'll do it two nights on both our patrol shifts. We'll make them sorry they made us patrol Sergeants."

Jesse never mentioned this crazy Randy plan on his date with Erin. The dinner was great and the movie predicable. They had an agreement that they wouldn't talk shop unless it was a mental health emergency. Even then, they set a 30-minute time limit. Erin believed that when you talked work, you were working without pay and that was dumb.

Jesse caught her when they were in the narc squad room.

"Hey Sergeant Beautiful."

"Watch the sex harassment Corporal Hunk."

Jesse smiled, "I'm supposed to brief you on a plan Cam, Randy and I are working on. Got a minute?"

"Why am I nervous before you even explain it? Ya, go ahead."

Jesse ran it all down and Erin just listened in silence.

"We could get kicked out of patrol before we even get trained well."

Jesse, faking surprise, said, "That's what Cam said."

"Jesse, what did Lieutenant Glen say about this idea?"

"Nothing, he doesn't know."

Friday night rolled around and patrol division, with the help of traffic division, set up a sobriety check point on a major traffic route in the city. The traffic officers were told once it started that a few narcs would be on hand with dogs, but that they should do the check point the way they normally do. Erin let Jesse run the operation with Randy's help. Traffic division did most of the work and they had drug recognition experts to test any suspects who were under the influence. All Jesse needed to do was get involved if the dogs alerted. By the end of the shift they had arrested 6 DUI for alcohol and 3 DUI for drugs, 12 people for possession of a controlled substance and 4 people for illegal possession of a loaded and concealed firearm. The whole operation was repeated on Saturday when Cam was pulling a patrol shift. Jesse just did a repeat in a different area. The arrest rate was remarkably similar.

Randy was ecstatic. Jesse was surprised. Cam was curious how else this could be used. And Lieutenant Glen was pissed.

CHAPTER 7

Glen stuck his head in the narc squad room, "Cam, my office." As he walked out, everyone looked at Cam and wondered if he'd survive this one.

Cam grabbed a cup of coffee, to project the casual look, and slowly strolled into the Lieutenant's office.

"Yes, Lieutenant?"

Glen wasn't a man that eased into things slowly, "DUI check point and dope dogs? Explain."

Cam smiled, "Oh, you wanted to know about my patrol division operation. Okay."

Glen frowned because he knew when he was being played.

Cam explained the operation and the legal thinking surrounding it.

"I really didn't think you'd want to know about a patrol activity, so you could have some deniability."

"Glen asked, "Did you inform Patrol Lieutenant Bledsoe about this?"

"He has all the reports, but if you're asking did I do it before hand, no."

Glen rubbed both his eyes with the palms of his hands and leaned back in his chair. "Well, I guess I'll make this his problem because I have enough of my own. A patrol operation, huh. I like that. He was whining for Sergeants a few months ago, let's see how he likes having my pack of maniacs."

"Cam sit," Glen pointed to a chair.

As, Cam sat down Glen said, "What other surprises do you have for me?"

Then, Cam explained his parolee surveillance idea.

∞

Erin went to work at the narc squad and was reviewing some search warrant drafts that two new narcs had written up. They were well done because both of the cops had years of police experience and the computer program made sure you didn't forget anything. Once she approved them, they'd find a judge to sign off.

It was late afternoon when Anna Sims and Bob Volk walked in her office.

"Sergeant Fulham, are you busy?"

Erin looked up, "You guys lost? No, come on in."

Anna started, "We're going on shift in a few minutes, but since you won't be back for a few days we wanted to let you know what we found out on the 261PC case with Gwen Abbott. We didn't figure it should wait."

"Okay, what's up?" Erin sat her paperwork aside and leaned forward on her arms.

"Bob did a check of the bar and several other similar bars for activity like this and came up with multiple suspicious attempts to adulterate drinks. Several bouncers threw guys out for what they thought was suspicious activity. We've got some general descriptions and it looks like it might be at least three guys. It's all being typed up now for a report.

I checked with detectives assigned to the sexual assault unit and they've had several similar reports, but have been too swamped with violent rapes and child molests to break anyone free to investigate the leads. They offered me the use of all their 290 PC pervert registrant books if I wanted to show photos to my victims and the bouncers. Anyway, it looks like we have an active roofie rapist group working and there's not much being done about it. The lab test came back positive for rohypnol."

Erin nodded, "Well, I guess we'll take the lead on this till someone tells me they got it. We'll send reports to sex crimes and hope their case load clears up, but I'm not willing to let these assholes operate in the meanwhile."

Bob and Anna nodded their agreement.

"Okay guys, let draft an action plan. We don't have to do everything ourselves. I can tap a few narcs to help since it involves dope. By the way, good job."

∞

Captain Johnson made one of his rare visits to the narc side of the building, so everyone knew it was serious.

He walked into to Lieutenant Glen's office and said, "Lieutenant, do you have a minute?" Then he sat down in front of Glen's desk. It really wasn't a question. It was more of an order.

Glen, understanding the message, answered correctly, "Absolutely, Captain." He got up and shut the door.

"Bud, explain to me your program involving narcs doing dog and gun searches at DUI check points."

Glen had to approach this gently. "Well, Captain, I was under the impression that the DUI function was a patrol activity. Their patrol Sergeant Cam Michaelson decided to add the dog component."

"Bud, are you trying to deflect your personnel's action off on other divisions?"

"Captain, it was an activity that was scheduled when he was under Lieutenant Bledsoe's supervision. There's no doubt he brought along some of his narc tactics, but I was not in charge of that operation."

"Bud, there were narcs all over that DUI post."

"Assisting patrol."

"I think you're toying with me, splitting this mess to suit the political winds. Let me ask you, will you be submitting those arrests made out there as part of your division's arrest stats?"

Glen cracked an ear-to-ear smile and said, "Of course."

Captain Johnson couldn't help but smile, "You're really gonna break it off in them for stealing your Sergeants, aren't you?"

"Absolutely." The Captain walked out the door.

Thirty minutes later Lieutenant Glen's phone rang. "Bud, this is Jim Bledsoe. What the fuck are your people doing to me?"

CHAPTER 8

Cam was dangerously close to using his black belt karate skills and both guns he carried. He was so angry he thought that after he broke this pile of crap into pieces with his bare hands, he would empty his weapon into what was left. IKEA was a huge Swedish conspiracy to drive other countries insane, so they could be conquered without a fight. Russia, China, North Korea, they weren't the problem, it was the Swedes.

Jane found it amusing and wasn't sympathetic at all to his complaints. "Here, have a beer and relax. It's just baby furniture. How hard could that be?"

He couldn't wait to go back to work where the only problems were people shooting at him.

∞

Bobby walked into the Tuesday morning meeting a little late. He was forgiven because he brought donuts.

"There's a granola bar in there somewhere for you Cam."

Cam frowned at him a grabbed a maple bar. He wasn't a complete fanatic.

"What ya got, Bobby?"

"I met with Data and he came up with some programs that we can use. I called him last week and gave him an overview of our idea, so he searched around and downloaded some free-- at least I think they were free-- computer programs.

These are information sheets. We fill them out on each parolee, feed them into the program and it will spit out probability along with some hard data on what he's likely to do, maybe even how and when."

Erin said, "Sounds like profiling to me."

Bobby smiled, "It is, but it never asks about race or religion. It asks questions like previous arrest charges, partners, weapons, times, days of the week, drugs, alcohol, vehicles, residences and tons of other MO factors. Some of them are unusual, they're not the type of things you'd think were predictors, but apparently, they are. It even has a place to log comments by parole officers that they boil down to a few descriptions. After it's all said and done the results just give you statistical likelihoods of occurrence and it really relies on us to make the educated guess where and when it's going to happen."

Cam offered, "So then we're back to code 5's and old fashion investigations?"

Bobby agreed, "Yep."

Cam asked, "So, who can we get to load all this information? It's likely to suck up a few days."

Erin offered, "I've got a couple of seniors that help out in the office during my patrol shift as volunteers. They're really sharp older ladies and if I explain this to them, I think they'll be glad to help."

Bobby said, "Let me put this in some kind of order so it makes sense to them, then I'll get it to you."

Cam asked about other issues or investigations.

Erin told them where she was on the roofie rapes and Cam explained the political fallout from his DUI check point arrests.

He said, "The irony is nobody said not to do it anymore, so I think wave two will happen in a couple of weeks. I might even add a twist Randy dreamed up."

He dismissed the meeting before anybody could ask what it was.

∞

Placing Erin and Cam in a one day a week patrol Sergeant's position was having a disruptive effect on the normal uniformed division operation. It wasn't that they did anything wrong exactly; it was more like they did things differently.

The other patrol Sergeants didn't like it either. The new kids on the block were ruffling everybody's feathers.

Lieutenant Glen kind of liked different.

Captain Johnson could tolerate different, but Lieutenant Bledsoe hated different when it ambushed him.

Ambitious law enforcement managers all knew that promotions were based on lack of waves. Chiefs like managers that don't make waves. Creative, aggressive, and innovative cops always received attention, but the best way to survive and promote was to remain boring and predictable. Plus, the innovative cops occasionally made mistakes. It was the price of adventure. In every boat race someone gets wet.

Erin plugged Anna Sims into being a training officer for Cam's problem rookie. She was a probationary officer just out of the academy. Jeanna Barker was personable, physically fit and was actively recruited because the department needed women. She did not, however, possess one important quality all cops need. She was not at all brave. Policework is full of people that are scared. That's not a problem. In fact, the absence of fear means you're crazy and it will probably get you killed. The thing that's needed is to overcome the fear and take action. The more experience an officer gets, the easier it is for them to do it. Jeanna wasn't progressing and all her FTO's felt like she never would. They believed she just wasn't cut out for a job in law enforcement. The problem was when males made that judgement call on females, it was often seen as macho male intolerance. That's where Anna came in. She had proven herself repeatedly and didn't have much patience with women who couldn't measure up. Anna knew that generally speaking women had trouble matching men in physical strength and fighting ability, but she knew that as long as you were there for a fellow officer and gave your full effort, the guys would accept you.

What Anna hated about some women is that they made an almost Darwinist adaptation when confronted with force or violence. They used their feminine power of influence to get men to do their physical work. It was one thing to flirt, but it was not okay to get the male officers to make your arrests because you were afraid. She failed women for that, quickly. Anna knew that the male officers were quick to place women in a category. If you couldn't do police work without being propped up then maybe you could be good for sex or cookies. The macho police culture could force women into the whore or mother role almost accidently. Anna wasn't about to let that happen when she was in charge. All of this was a political mine field, that administrators ran away from. It was easier to just pass the women that were marginal and get the female officer percentage up on the force. That appeased city hall and got everybody off your butt. Many agencies solved the problem of unsuited women on patrol by making them detectives. That way they could get others to make their arrests and the violence inherent in patrol work was minimized. That pissed off male patrolmen because they were passed over for detective positions for people who couldn't do their job.

And on some occasions, female recruits were discriminated against just because they were female. That's why all this was a mine field.

Cam looked up from his desk to see Officer Anna Sims standing in front of him. She had an irritated look on her face as she waited for him to acknowledge her.

"Yes, Anna. What's up?"

"I've finished that training report you wanted." She dropped a file on his desk.

"Okay, I'll look it over and thanks."

She added, "I don't like being the one that gets all of these."

Cam recognized that she felt used, was hot tempered and could easily say something rash if provoked.

"I know how you feel. I always get called when they need a karate guy to kick someone's ass. Just three weeks ago they arrested a lineman for the Raiders for DUI and I happened to be in the booking area. The Lieutenant on duty called me into the booking room and told me that this 290 lb. 6-foot 5 guy wouldn't take off his Super Bowl ring for processing."

"He says, 'use some of that Kung Fu bullshit of yours and get that ring.' Keep in mind, this football tackle is a specialist at tolerating pain and inflicting it."

"So, I asked him, 'Lieutenant, why do we take rings from prisoners before we jail them?'"

"He puffs up and says, 'so that other inmates don't steal them from the prisoner.'"

"I looked at him and pointed to this monster and said, 'be serious, do you think anybody is going to fuck with him?'"

"The Lieutenant throws up his hands and says, 'Oh, never mind.'"

Cam leaned back in his chair and smiled at the now smiling Anna.

She said, "Nice pivot, Sergeant."

Cam nodded, "I'll try to spread these unpleasant training evals around, so they don't all end up in your lap. You do know that the reason we use you is because you're respected, don't you?"

She rolled her eyes and waved with only her fingers as she turned to leave Cam's office, "Erin told me you were smooth."

Cam read Anna's report which relied on four other trainers' assessment that the trainee wasn't cutting it. She did a synopsis that basically concurred. She added that she was on alert for gender bias and found none. In fact, she criticized her male counterparts for extending too much latitude because they were afraid of being judged intolerant. She gave several specific examples of fear driven decisions that could get someone hurt, especially the trainee herself. The trainee would be fired after all the investment of money time and effort by both her and the department. The waste was frustrating and sad, but that was how the system worked. The goal was everybody's safety.

Cam had enough of reading and making unpleasant decisions for one night. He hit Terrence on the air, "One Adam 17, S6."

"Go ahead S6."

"Ready for that 10-10?"

"Affirmative, ETA 5."

Cam double clicked the mic to acknowledge. Going to coffee with Terrence was always like a breath of mental fresh air.

Cam and Terrence liked to have coffee at a small mom and pop cafe near the 101 freeway. Terrence had helped the owner's kid out of a legal jam and got him into the Marine Corps. The result was a proud family that would walk through fire for Terrence. They brought Cam and Terrence coffee and returned with a slice of pie for both of them.

Cam declined the pie but Terrence said, "Quiet now, I think someone will eat that pie."

Terrence asked Cam about his pending family. Cam and Jane had completed the adoption, so he had one kid, but with Jane pregnant with twins he was about to be a family man with a capital F.

"I'm scared to death Terrence. Any advice?"

Terrence laughed and said, "Jane will tell you everything you need to do and then some. Us guys, we just listen, smile and pack a lot of crap around. Clean and haul. Most women have instincts that get them through it all. We got to wait for them to grow. The women, they got a nine-month jump on us. But I've got to tell you, it's the most important thing I've ever done. You're making a human being from scratch. Are they gonna be smart, kind and decent? Will they be happy and healthy? Will you like them? You got to love em, but you don't have to like em. That's where just being with them and doing stuff together matters. That quality time theory was made up by guilty parents who don't spend enough time with their kids. It's not possible for some parents, I know that, but guys like us can find the time. My kids are my best friends. I love being with them and teaching them about life. I want them to have all the skills to be happy and independent when they leave the nest. You and Jane are solid folk, you'll do fine. Now, gimme that piece of pie since you're just gonna stare at it."

Cam slid the plate of pie toward Terrence and smiled. He felt better. Terrence should get a couch and charge by the hour.

Terrence was giving Cam a ride back to the station when dispatch announced a large fight at a bowling alley restaurant. They had dispatched several cars, but were short officers because several other units were handling other calls, so Terrence and Cam responded.

When Cam went through the front door, he saw four officers trying to arrest a dozen combatants. He and Terrence waded into the fight grabbing suspects to cuff. Cam hit a large half-drunk guy with an open hand on his left shoulder spinning him around as Cam grabbed his right jacket sleeve to help with the turn. The drunk was cuffed quickly and as Cam was getting ready to remove him another drunk took a swing at Cam's head. Cam deflected the blow up and punched the suspect in the solar plexus, removing the guy's wind. Cam did a leg sweep dumping him on his back on the floor. He handed his first prisoner to a reserve that was hauling suspects to his patrol car, grabbed the kid's cuffs and proceeded to cuff the prone suspect he'd punched. He grabbed a wrist, jerked the guy's arm straight out, then flipped him just like he was a pancake. When he'd cuffed him, he sat him up and walked him to the transport unit. Cam and his officers had everyone arrested and were sorting out who was the report writer on this call. Once they identified the responsible officer, Cam told him he'd write a report on the two guys he arrested.

Terrence said, "Come on Sergeant, you've had enough fun for the night." He gave him a ride back to the office.

Cam felt much better. A chat with Terrence and a painless fight was just what he needed.

Just before Cam was ready to go home, the front desk officer called him.

"S6, we have a citizen who just bailed out, at the front desk with a personnel complaint."

"10-4, I'll be up in a minute."

When Cam arrived at the front desk, he recognized the half-drunk fighter he'd dropped to the floor with a leg sweep.

The guy stepped over to meet Cam and introduced himself. "Sergeant, I'm John Dorn and one of your officers' sucker punched me in the gut and kicked me to the ground. When he had me down, he put the boot to me. Stomped me bad."

Cam had to fight a grin because this guy was so wasted, he didn't recognize Cam as the guy who arrested him.

Cam said, "Really? Step over to this desk Mr. Dorn and let me get some information." It suddenly dawned on Cam that he hadn't had the cleaners sew Sergeants stripes on his cold weather jacket yet, so when he was in the bowling alley, he had nothing on his uniform that would identify him as a Sergeant.

Cam took a detailed report from the Mr. Dorn which was full of exaggerations and outright lies.

After he completed it asked, "Okay Mr. Dorn would you like to sign this complaint under penalty of perjury?" he spun the report around and handed Dorn a pen.

Mr. Dorn said, "Well, I really don't know if that's a good idea. It might be a perjury trap. I've been hearing a lot about those lately."

Cam said, "Well, that does limit what I can do with this information. What is it you'd like to see happen here? Would you be satisfied if I just had a good conversation with this officer and straightened him out?"

Bob Dorn said, "I guess that would be okay. I just don't want this shit to happen to anybody else."

He and Cam stood up and Mr. Dorn shook Cam's hand, "Thank you Sergeant, you're really a good guy."

Mr. Dorn walked out the front door and Cam walked back to his office. He dropped the report in his office trash can, announcing to no one, "Fucking moron."

CHAPTER 9

Erin, Anna and Bob sat down after briefing and worked up an action plan.

Erin started by saying, "Look guys, this is all new to me, so any suggestions you have would be helpful."

Bob spoke first. "I've been thinking about this case and I don't think showing the 290-registrant book to the victims is going to net us anything except frustrated victims. Guys that pull shit like this are usually young and first offenders. I think Anna and I should split up the bars that cater to youngsters and try and get a description of the guys they've kicked out or thought were up to something."

Anna added, "We need to re-interview all the victims detectives talked with and see if we can come up with any MO factors like night of the week or time."

Erin said, "Sounds good and if we get some descriptions and places to look, we can use some of my narcs to pull code 5's there."

"Anna, try to pull all of the detective reports and ours. See if you can make some sense out of all these loose ends."

"Bob, we might ask some of the bouncers and bartenders who the regulars are. I'll bet some of the ladies that patronize these places can tell you who the creeps are, and you might just warn some of them, so they don't become victims."

Everybody agreed this was a good plan, so Erin wrote it up and would give Bob and Anna copies.

"You two feel free to touch base with me when I'll across the building working narcotics if you get anything."

It was four days before Anna and Bob came across the building and met with Erin.

They both had a confident grin.

Anna started, "Okay Sarge, here's what we came up with. We have three bars where the bartender and several ladies have noticed some slime-balls attempting to get women alone. The bouncers kicked one guy out of a bar because they thought he was stealing women's drinks, but we figure he was up to other stuff."

Bob interrupted, "And, we think we have several MO factors that could help."

Erin was jazzed, "Yes! Okay let me hear it all."

Bob and Anna gave Erin a lot of information that was actionable. Based on the apparent MO factors and descriptions, she was able to set up a stake out schedule for the narc squad. She felt like Jesse was a good coordinator for this detail because he had some sex crime investigation experience and was a Corporal. She would handle the overall investigation.

Jesse had two officers set up on each of three bars from 11:00 pm to closing at 2:00 am, this was when Bob and Anna said the MO factors indicated the crooks were active. The stake out officers had physical descriptions that included height, weight, clothes and a few other traits on three possible suspects.

Tommy was assigned to Randy at a bar called the "Hot Spot."

Tommy asked Jesse, "So, this means I get to drink beer and chase women, right? And the city is buying, right?"

Jesse looked back over his shoulder, "That's right, junior. Just make sure you're stone sober if you make an arrest."

Jesse told everyone, "I'll be with Todd and Al is working with Anna. This is her normal night off, but she's pulling OT with us tonight because she's been working this investigation for a couple of weeks."

After a four-hour shift the squad packed it in for the night. Back at the squad room Erin asked, "Anything happen tonight?'

Jesse said, "Tommy got two hot phone numbers and Randy came up with an idea for salty crackers that serve as edible bar coasters."

Erin shook her head in amazement of the never-ending volume of craziness flowing from Randy's head. "Okay guys, tomorrow night, same teams, same bars. Anna, you want to burn through your other free night?"

"Yes, I do the bar scene for free usually."

Everyone laughed and went home.

The next night everybody was well into their stakeout shift when Al and Anna both noticed a guy that fit the description given by one of the bartenders.

He was talking with a girl at the bar even though she was trying to give him a polite brush off. They were watching her drink and his hands like a hawk while trying not to look too suspicious. The suspect backed off of his target and acted low key, occasionally commenting on something to her.

Anna shoved her chair closer to Al and cupped her hand to his ear.

"He ordered the same drink as her when he was drinking beer. I'll bet he'll add the dope to his drink giving it time to dissolve, then switch glasses. It's easier than adding it to her drink."

Al noticed that he drank his drink till it was the same level as the girl's, then he watched her in the bar mirror as he also kept an eye on the bartender. The suspect had his hand across the top of his glass and easily could have dropped something into it.

Sure enough, as soon as she turned away and the bartender wasn't looking, he put his hand over the top of his drink and set it down right next to hers. He picked up her drink and turned away.

Anna looked at Al and motioned with her head toward the suspect and victim.

Al leaned over and said into her ear, "Not yet."

After about 15 minutes went by, it was obvious that the girl was drugged. The suspect was now standing beside her talking and holding her up. She looked like she would fall off the stool had he not been leaning against her. Ten minutes later he was walking her out of the bar.

As Al and Anna followed, he told Anna, "Get the bartender to set those two glasses aside for us, then meet me in the parking lot."

Anna walked up to the bartender and badged him, "I need you to save those two glasses for me. Don't empty them, they're evidence." The bartender set them on a high shelf behind the bar.

As Anna ran out the door, she saw Al walk up to the suspect and say, "Hey, dude, what's up with my roommate there? Guess she got a little hammered tonight, huh? You weren't gonna take her to your place were ya? My girlfriend and I will handle it from here." Al grabbed the girl's arm and took her away from the suspect.

Anna wasn't sure what Al was doing, but since they were undercover and Al didn't identify himself as a cop, she figured he was staying undercover for some reason, so she kept her mouth shut and helped Al take the girl to their car.

The suspect, Brian Defoe said, "Man, I was just helping her to her car to sleep it off. I wasn't doing nothin'."

Al ignored him and put the girl in the back seat of the undercover car.

The girl was passed out and laying on the seat as Anna and Al got in the front.

"Okay Al, what the fuck?"

"Chill, Anna. We got this asshole. We'll cop his plates and follow him till he goes home. The problem we have with this case is there are three suspects and arresting him won't help us ID the other two. He'll clam up and then we've only got a piece of the group. If we let him walk, we'll surveil him till we see who his friends are. We can get his phone info and see who he talks with. This is the old investigate or arrest decision all cops have to make. If no one is getting hurt, it's still better to investigate and get the other accomplices."

"So, what do we do with her?"

Al smiled and said, "We'll take her by the hospital and get her some help shortly. They'll also get some blood for us which will be good evidence. I need to get some of the other guys to help follow our crook, then we can break away."

"N22, N26."

"Go ahead 26."

"I'm following one of our suspects and need help with a rolling surveillance."

"We'll be there in 10. Update me on your 10-20 as we go."

Al answered, "10-4."

Anna and Al followed the suspect at a distance after they drove by his car and ran the plates. Brian Defoe was a 25-year-old local boy who lived on Palm Ave. in San Jose. A quick records check showed he had priors for theft and assault. The original charges were burglary and assault with a deadly weapon, but he plea bargained them down to misdemeanors. It looked like he was heading home, so that let Al loosen his surveillance and not get burned.

Tommy and Randy hooked up with Al down the street from the suspect's house.

Al told Tommy, "You guys keep an eye on our friend and see if he has any company tonight. I think it's too late for him to work any more bars, but you never know."

Tommy asked, "What you gonna do with this victim?"

"Anna and I will run her over to the hospital and then we'll call Erin to see how she wants to handle this thing."

Tommy added, "This girl doesn't know how close she came to being a rape victim tonight. She'll probably never go into a bar the rest of her life."

Anna said, "No shit. It was so smooth and quick Al and I barely saw it."

They ran the girl to the hospital and explained to the ER doctor what had happened. He said he'd do a full blood work-up on the victim, so he'd know how to treat her. Al knew he'd need a warrant to get the results, but that was standard. He was positive they'd find rohypnol.

Al phoned Erin, "I've got Tommy and Randy sitting on the house with the suspect and we just dropped the victim off at emergency. We're going to swing back by the bar and collect the glasses they were using, for evidence. I'll get the lab to give us a quick check for roofies. The hospital will test her blood, because they need it for treatment. We can either get a waiver from the victim or a warrant for the test results."

Erin said, "Good, now we have to figure out how...........stand by."

"N26 22."

Al answered, "Go ahead N22."

"We have another vehicle that just pulled into the driveway with two white male occupants. I think we're going to need help covering this place if somebody leaves."

Erin broke into the conversation, "N units this N8. N18 what's your status?"

Jesse answered, "N8, we're in route to N22's location, ETA 15."

"Erin asked, "N units copy?"

There was a series of double clicks indicating they got the message.

Todd was driving, so Jesse said, "Drop me three houses away. I'll walk by the house and get the license plate number. Write it down when I give it to you over the air. I'm too senile to remember it."

"Will do."

Jesse walked by the house and keyed his radio mic clipped to his jacket lapel. "California APJ926, Adam, Paul, John, 926."

It came back registered to a suspect that lived very close by. Jesse and Todd met with Tommy and Randy and worked out a plan to watch these three guys.

"N8, N18."

"Go ahead N18."

Jesse explained to Erin what he was doing at the stakeout and they agreed that they would sit on the house for a few more hours before leaving. An hour later, which was nearing 3:00 am the car that arrived at the suspect Defoe's house left. It had the same two guys in the vehicle. They went back to their residence about seven blocks away and after 15 minutes all the lights went out.

Jesse called Erin on his phone because he figured this to be a longer conversation and didn't want to tie up air traffic with head scratching.

"Well, Erin, I figure they're down for the night. Tommy tells me his guy turned off all the lights too."

"Ya, I think we can shut it down. I ran the RO for the plate you called in. The registered owner is Bradley Pope, 24, who's got a few priors. He's also got a brother who lives with him: Tyler Pope, 19, and he's got a few also. We just might have IDed the three suspects in this group. Now, all we need to do is get some good photos of these three schmucks and run some photo lineups. If we can get some positive IDs, we'll get warrants. Why don't you send all our troops home and I'll get someone on days to follow up with getting more background on these suspects and the photos we'll need. We'll show the pictures to bartenders and victims tomorrow. Correction, later today."

Jesse said, "10-4 Sergeant, sleep sounds good right now. You coming over?"

"Okay."

"Wake me."

"Oh ya."

CHAPTER 10

Cam and Bobby were looking over the computer data that the senior volunteers had fed into the program. Once all the information was loaded, it only took seconds for the program to project future occurrences based on past occurrences. Bobby was writing down notes and dissecting all the information.

"Well, Bobby, what's that savant computer brain of yours tell you?"

"These three guys are gonna do it all over again, just like they did the last time they were caught. They've screwed up every time they were turned loose and the computer says that since nothing significant in their personal life has changed, such as getting married, sick, or injured and they still haven't reached criminal menopause, which is 40 years old. They'll do it again."

"Okay, who am I to argue? I'll call Danny Dominquez and see what he has to say." Cam told Danny what the computer program spit out and asked for his opinion.

"Sounds about right, especially the prediction about Juan Ortiz. He's a crazy MF. When I meet with him, he doesn't even try to hide the fact that he thinks it's all bull. His record is full of violence and a PO that had him previously advised me to always take backup when I deal with him. So, how you guys going to work this?"

Cam confessed, "I'm not sure. We're making this shit up as we go. Thanks Danny, I'll be in touch."

Cam walked over to Bobby's desk, "Come on, I'll buy you lunch and we can talk."

Bobby jumped up, "First time ever! Let's go."

Cam drove out to a park on their old beat, when they were patrol partners and jumped the curb with the undercover car. He drove to the top of a grassy hill and reached into the back seat for his ice chest.

Bobby started laughing, "I knew it was too good to be true. Don't tell me, now that you're a family man you can't afford to eat out anymore."

Cam smiled, "That's about right. Do you know how much babies cost today? What am I saying? I'm asking a Mormon if he knows what babies cost. Say, do your people get a discount for volume, cause I could use a break with this twofer twin thing?"

"You're a funny man, Cam. It's gonna be sweet laughing my butt off at you packing around high chairs, diaper bags, play pens, and all the other assorted must-have baby paraphernalia. Pretty soon the center console of your car will be full of baby wipes and pacifiers. Oh, I forgot to mention, a guy at my church has a great used van for sale. Should I get his number for you? Cause all those dependents won't fit in your sports car."

Cam shook his head, "You're loving this shit, aren't you?"

Bobby belly laughed, "Yes!"

Cam handed him the ice chest and Booby pulled out a sandwich and a cold drink.

They started eating and both of them started laughing again.

Bobby commented, "Lot of changes since we used to eat here, huh?"

"Ya. Times were simpler then."

#

"Okay Bobby, to business. How should we set this up?"

Bobby rubbed his neck as he twisted his head from side to side, "How about we prioritize these three guys, 1, 2, 3, and have our narcs stake them out as time allows. This could be our default activity when our guys have some down time. This detail isn't the kind of thing we can just set someone on for an indefinite stakeout, because we really don't have probable cause to believe a crime is being committed, right?"

Cam nodded, "Right, Lieutenant Glen isn't going to go for me pulling everybody off real cases and speculating on these crimes that might go down. So, we need a supervisor that clears everyone for stakeout duty."

Bobby agreed, "Ya, I could set it up and then whoever is a working supervisor could log on and assign officers as needed."

"So, Bobby, what would that look like?"

"Well, all the Sergeants and Corporals would just log on to the site where they'll find our three crooks listed as suspects 1-2-3 with a full description of them and all the personal data like house, car, family, friends, and all the safety stuff like priors and danger factors. We'd have a calendar where we could type in the narcs or officers assigned to code 5's and we'd keep a log entry of what they saw, like vehicle plates, visitors, or anything important. We could also have a spot to write DB (drive by) info for cops just patrolling past the crooks."

"So, for example, Tommy's got some slack, we log on and tell him, go to suspect 2 and code 5 for a few hours, then enter what you saw in the site."

Cam was once again amazed at how creative Bobby was. "This sounds pretty good. I could have my patrol officer do occasional drive bys and forward info to me. I wouldn't give them the log on because that's just too many people writing on the site, but they could get plate numbers and note strange activity."

Bobby nodded, "Uniforms always hate the fact that narcs don't share information even when we spring their arrests to make them informants. This could help bridge that sharing gap. It would show we trust them."

"Ya, you're right, but we'll have to remind them that they're driving marked units, so be careful not to burn the surveillance."

Bobby added, "When and if we start to get the picture that a crime is gonna go down, we'll have to shift into another gear."

"Ya, maybe I'll put Jesse on that. We need a tactical plan for a 211 (robbery) scenario and chances are we're not going to get much lead time."

"You gonna talk with Glen about this?"

"Yes, potential gun battles are the kind of thing he needs to know about, but I won't do it till you have the log-in coordination site up and running. That will impress him and maybe he won't think I'm just being a crazy shit once again."

Bobby laughed, "Even though you are."

∞

The log-in site worked great. Erin had her patrol shift tracking all three 211 suspects and providing her with information to put into the database. The whole narc squad found it a productive way of using time when they were waiting for court, burning a few hours till a warrant was served or a shift ended. As the information rolled in Bobby had it added to the crook's database and then re-ran the program to see if it updated any predictions. Everything was working like it was supposed to. Even Lieutenant Glen was impressed, and not much impressed him.

While all this was going on, Jesse, with the help of Randy, was getting some tactical equipment and procedures squared away. He had decided after talking with Lieutenant Tomasovic, the SWAT commander, that it wasn't always possible to get the big guns to every crime in progress. It took a little time for them to deploy, so Tomasovic recommended that a few of the narcs get qualified to carry specialized weapons. This included assault rifles, chemical agent guns and a few other toys. Todd was first in line to volunteer. Jesse would need a couple more, although his real desire was to have SWAT handle the hot crimes in progress.

CHAPTER 11

Juan Ortiz wasn't a unique criminal. He had at least two names he used depending on the situation, and while he was technically a citizen of the United States parole didn't know his full background because that was the way he liked it. He was born in the United States but raised in Tijuana by his father. His mother lived in San Diego where he and his dad visited regularly, but she wouldn't move to Tijuana because it was too dangerous. Juan's dad was a gang member and the violence that surrounded him was constant and terrifying to most people. Juan's mother begged him to let her raise the boy away from the gang life, but the macho rules that Juan's father lived by required a man to raise a son to be strong and tough. It worked. Juan was a hard-core gang member who never hesitated to use violence when provoked. The only reason he'd never served a murder sentence is because he'd never been caught. When he moved to San Jose at the request of his gang leader, it was to eliminate a boss that had been skimming from the drug sales profits. Juan was told to make the hit memorable, so that everyone knew what would happen if they stole from the gang. One day when the target had been relaxing after a few beers in a wooden chair on the gang's back yard patio, Juan walked up behind him with half of a 5-gallon bucket containing gasoline and poured it over his body putting the bucket over the guy's head. As the target was trying to get the bucket off and get up, Juan lit a match and threw it on his chest. The combustion and 10-foot fire ball were jaw dropping. The target fell back where he was seated as the flame consumed the body and burned the wooden Adirondack chair.

Everyone was in shock as Juan yelled, "Let him burn! This thief stole from the gang and if you don't want to die like this, don't steal from us." Juan's position and reputation were cemented in the gang after that.

Juan had been cooped up in prison for five long years and was angry as hell that he had to start over when he joined the San Jose branch. After the thief barbeque, he was elevated to be gang leader, but the San Jose gang members didn't know him, so he had to make sure they showed sufficient respect. Killing the previous leader was a good start, but he had to lead by example to gain their loyalty. That meant he had to be in on a few shootings and robberies to show he wasn't afraid of going back to prison. He was, but he couldn't show it. Weakness gets your killed in the gang world, and there were four other guys who thought they'd be in line to lead the gang when the time came. Any one of them was a threat.

Juan was planning a robbery of a grocery store. It would cement his leadership with the gang because the take would be huge. They would hit the store early Monday morning of a three-day weekend. He had all the details worked out because he'd done it before. The last time he did it six years ago, he'd been caught in the parking lot because the wheel man fucked up and wasn't in the correct place. The cops happened to be close by when the call came in. He had plans to fix those problems. For five years he'd laid in his bunk at night and thought about how they'd messed up and what he should have done to pull it off correctly. He'd thought it all through and this time it would go down perfectly. But this time he'd have to cover his face completely instead of just wear sunglasses and a hat. He got some face and neck tattoos in prison that would have to be covered.

CHAPTER 12

Erin's case against the three roofie rapists was building nicely. The lab results all came in positive for rohypnol. She had Anna and Bob show an assortment of people a photo lineup with the three suspect's photos included. Bar patrons, bartenders and victims identified the three as being in the bars and close to the victims when they were drugged.

Erin called Bob and Anna in for an update, "I'm going to get warrants for the two houses and we'll plan a raid. Are you two up for a little OT (overtime)?"

Both of them said they were interested.

The warrant affidavit included the original rape of Gwen Abbott and the reported rapes the detectives had cases on. Also, Erin added the stakeout surveillance by Anna and Al, as well as the lab reports. The judge didn't hesitate.

"Good luck Sergeant. Sounds like we have some nasty predators working."

Erin set up the raid during her and Cam's normal narcotic squad workday at 7:00 am. That way they would hopefully catch everybody at home and in bed. Erin made squad assignments since it was her case. She was going to hit Brian Defoe's house with Bobby, Al, Anna Sims and Tommy. Cam would hit the Pope brothers with Jesse, Todd, Bob Volk and Randy. They needed to hit the houses simultaneously to avoid the other house being warned about the raid. Because of the identification problem it was critical that they find incriminating evidence. The case had problems if they had to rely on eyewitness testimony. The drugged state of the victims made it a difficult case. The last victim, Kimberly Short, was not actually raped and the previous ones didn't have evidence-based proof of a rape. There was no rape kit or eyewitness. That made the case a challenge for the District Attorney's Office.

These guys weren't your typical gun-toting thugs, so the squad executed a low-profile service. Both Cam and Erin covered all the exits but left their guns holstered during the Knock and Notice. They identified themselves as police officers and explained they had a search warrant. The occupants of both houses told the officers that they were sure this was some type of big mistake.

Cam hit Erin on the air.

"N8, N6, status?"

Erin answered, "N8, inside secure and searching."

"10-4, same here. Let me know if you find anything."

Erin gave the mic a double click.

After two hours of searching Cam discovered a supply of rohypnol hidden under a bathroom sink. Randy had opened the cabinet door, laid down on his back and looked up around the edge of the sink using a flashlight. The crook had hammered in a small nail and had a Ziplock baggie full of around 200 roofies in the bag, hanging from the nail.

Cam looked at Randy and said, "Randy, how do you find shit like this? What made you look there?"

"Well Sarg, I just try and think about where I might hide something like that. It's got to be in a place I control like my room, but out of sight where anybody else might look and it's good if it's near a toilet for disposal. You also can't be afraid to get down on the ground once and a while."

Cam shook his head, "Well, whatever works. Good job." He slapped Randy on the back as he walked into the living room.

Bob and Jesse walked up to Cam, and Jesse said, "Cam, I think we need to call a tech on this guy's computer. If he has any pictures of the women he's been raping, they'll be on the computer and anything we do like unplug it or turn it on or off might wipe it according to Bob here." Bob nodded his agreement.

"Cam handed Jesse his portable radio and said, "Okay, call for one and we'll stand-by till they arrive. Get a transportation unit for Mr. Defoe and call Erin with a status report."

Jesse said, "10-4."

Cam continued to read documents and paperwork at the suspect's desk to see if he could find any information on where the drugs originated. While he was looking around waiting for the computer technician, he found some medical receipts that indicated the suspect had been tested for STD's on a regular basis every six months for the past three years. Cam got a sick feeling in his stomach. If this germaphobe felt the need for tests over the past three years, that just might be the length of this crime spree.

Cam walked up to Jesse, Bob and the tech. "What do you think?"

The tech had both the computer and printer secured and was ready to load it into his van. He said, "I think they'll be fine. It may take a while to crack them, but we'll get it done."

Cam asked, "Why the printer?"

"Cause it's a computer too, and may have some memory storage of anything printed."

Cam nodded, "Jesse, dial up your main squeeze on your phone and let me talk with her."

Jesse pulled out his cell and hit Erin's number.

"Yes?"

"Hey Sergeant, Cam needs a word." He handed the phone to Cam.

"Erin, let me explain where Randy found some dope because I think these boneheads are likely to share hiding information. Also, we seized a computer and a bunch of software, but I think this thing could be bigger than we originally thought."

Cam explained about the three-year medical history of the suspect.

Erin was quiet for a minute, "Shit, I hope you're wrong about this."

"Me too."

Erin walked past Anna and Tommy. "You two, follow me." As she walked to the rear of the house into the master bedroom, she explained the information relayed to her from Cam.

"I want you two to tear this place apart back here. Start with this sink and all the cabinets in the bathroom."

Ten minutes later Tommy found a baggie shoved in a crack under the sink, between the rim of the sink and the plywood cut out. It held about 150 roofies. Anna had pulled out a hair dryer and two folded towels from the bottom right-hand cabinet. She then peeled up an adhesive piece of shelf paper to discover someone had drilled a finger sized hole in the bottom and cut out an 18" square piece of the bottom with a jig saw. It could be removed by putting your finger in the hole and lifting up. It was sitting on four small blocks glued to the bottom of the hole lip so that when it was in place with the shelf paper over it, nothing unusual showed. Below was a four-inch air space where the cabinet sat on a frame that provided the inset all bathroom cabinets had that allowed users to step closer to the sink.

Tommy watched Anna remove the lid and pull out a two-inch-thick stack of standard   8 x 11-inch paper printed with photos of naked women passed out in cars and on beds, many being raped or otherwise molested.

Anna whispered, "Oh, sweet Jesus."

Tommy looked over her shoulder, and with a thumb and forefinger splayed several sheets of paper.

"Looks like they're all different victims. This case just became huge."

∞

As all the officers sat around the squad room and tried to get their heads around what they'd discovered. Everyone was in a mild state of shock.

Bobby started with, "I think we've got to pass this thing off to detectives. All these victims have to be identified and interviewed. This is a logistical nightmare."

Cam asked Erin, "What's the tentative victim count?"

"134."

Everyone was in stunned silence.

After a while Erin added, "The good news is after a cursory review, these assholes took pictures of themselves raping these women and didn't hide their faces. It appears that they used cell phones to take the pictures and downloaded them onto the computer. From there they copied them to make their little porn book."

Cam said, "Okay, give me any ideas you have and I'll talk with Lieutenant Glen. This thing just outgrew our little operation."

∞

Lieutenant Glen listened to Cam and Erin explain the rohypnol case with his feet crossed on the corner of his desk and his arms crossed on his stomach.

Glen commented, "Another byproduct of 21st century technology. Cell phone cameras, computer data storage, color printers, no film development require. Swell. Did you check to see if they put any of this stuff online for public viewing?"

Cam answered, "Our tech people are running some scans to see if they can find any pictures on amateur porn sites. They're also checking e-mails to see if the suspects have been sharing."

Erin added, "We didn't do a lot of stuff that should be done because we weren't sure how much would be done by us, given this is really a sexual assault investigation unit crime that detectives should handle."

Glen nodded, "Ya, I need to talk with the Detective Lieutenant and see what they have in mind. Have everybody get all their reports done and I'll get back to you as soon as Lieutenant Henderson and I talk."

∞

"Dick, Bud Glen."

"Hi Bud, I heard about the case you guys broke open. That was good work. Who's responsible for it?"

"Sergeant Erin Fulham and some of her officers from patrol division and narcotics."

"Don't suppose she'd like a detective assignment?"

"Don't you start poaching my people too."

Dick Henderson laughed, "Okay, how we gonna split this up?"

Glen paused and said, "Well, I was hoping you'd just take over because the current victim count is 134, and that's a lot of interviews if we can locate them."

"Well, I guess this is a detective responsibility. Is there anything you could pick up for us, because we're swamped over here?"

Glen thought for a few seconds, "I have a guy, Al Sylvester, that's a good interrogator. He did that gang member interview a while back that put away J-Tra. I'll have him do the suspect interviews and we'll chase down the rohypnol supply if possible. We've already done the search warrants on the houses and computers. That would leave the victim ID and interviews for your people."

"Bud, that sounds great. I appreciate all the help and give my congratulations to your people. They did one hell of a job."

Glen told Erin to get Al started on the interviews of the suspects. Technically it was an interrogation, but real world was, because of Miranda, you interviewed everyone. He updated her on his conversation with Lieutenant Henderson and told her to get someone on the rohypnol source after the interviews.

Erin waited for Glen to finish, "Lieutenant, the county felony task force might help detectives with the victim identification and interview part of this, especially since we can claim this is a multijurisdictional investigation."

"Good idea. Call Henderson and tell him that, and when he tries to get you to transfer to detectives, tell him, no."

Erin laughed, "10-4."

CHAPTER 13

Al was an experienced interrogator who knew all the tricks. You never screamed and yelled. You always got the subject talking and listened to his explanation of events. The suspect didn't rape anyone, he had sex with them. You didn't talk about the suspect's punishment, you made a friend of him, so he would talk and share his thoughts. You always interviewed the youngest or most vulnerable first and then you could share his statements with the others. It made them think lying was pointless. Mostly you downplayed the seriousness and listened rather than talked.

Al walked Tyler Pope out of the holding cell in cuffs. He bypassed the normal interrogation room and escorted the prisoner into a detective office he borrowed for a couple of hours. He took the cuffs off Tyler and told him to sit at an empty work table located in the room.

Al handed Tyler a cold Pepsi as he sat across from him and said, "Tyler, I need you to state your full name for my recording." Al set an audio recorder on the desk between them. After Tyler stated his name, Al pushed the recorder to the side so it wasn't directly in Tyler's view. Out of sight, out of mind.

"Tyler, I'm required to read you your rights, so just be patient while I go through this." Al read the Miranda warning in a low monotone voice with very little punctuation. He'd complied with the law, but set it up so Tyler really wasn't paying attention. If he had been, the phrase, "Anything you say can and will be used against you in court of law," should have told him to shut up. Tyler said he understood his rights and told Al he would talk with him. Most suspects do unless they had a prior arrest where a defense attorney chewed their ass for talking with the cops. Al started the interview by asking him his school and work history. He asked about how long he'd lived with his older brother and set up a conversation about how older brothers are kind of in charge. Al explained how his older brother used to get them in all kinds of shit.

Tyler laughed and said, "Ya, he's kind of the boss."

Al answered with, "Well, he probably should of left you out of this one." Tyler nodded. "So, when was the first time you got laid using the roofies?"

Tyler shrugged an, I don't know, so Al pressed, "A year ago? Three years ago? I see some of these pictures are from a couple years back." Al flipped through the print pictures Anna discovered under the bathroom cabinet floor, finding one with Tyler, "Was that your first sexual experience? I mean, were you a virgin before that?"

Tyler was insulted, "I wasn't no virgin. I had a steady girlfriend."

"Oh, okay, so you knew what was going on when you had sex with this girl in the picture?" Al had studied the rape pictures in the pile of photos and marked the ones with Tyler with a paper clip.

Tyler answered, "Ya."

"Did you give her a roofie or did someone else?"

He nervously said, "I didn't give her anything."

Tyler was locking up. He'd recognized the interview was getting into dangerous territory. The two essential elements to rape were sexual intercourse and lack of consent. A drugged woman can't give consent.

"Then was it your brother or Brian?" Tyler was quiet and thinking.

"Because either you did or they did. You're not gonna start lying to me are ya, Tyler?" Tyler folded his arms across his chest and Al could tell he was going to lock up on him, so he switched to another tactic. Al laid the stack of photos in front of Tyler and started to go through them slowly, one at a time, turning them over after he made comments or asked questions about each one. After they had gone through about 30 or 40 photos Tyler turned his head and didn't want to look at them anymore.

Al said, "Tyler, act like a man and tell me what you see here." Tyler looked back at the pictures. "Tell me how old you think this girl is Tyler, 15, maybe 16?"

Al was getting to a place in the stack of photos where the girls looked younger. "Where'd you guys meet these girls? They're not drinking age. Not in a bar."

As Al flipped through a few more pages Tyler slammed his hand down on a picture and screamed, "That mother fucker!"

Al was jolted out of his interview mode and almost punched Tyler because he thought he was going to be attacked, but then he realized Tyler was upset by the photo of a girl he apparently knew.

"Who is she Tyler? How do you know her?"

Tyler was tearing up. "She's my best friend's little sister. She and I dated a couple of times, then all of a sudden, she stopped talking to me. Now I know why. That fucker Brian must have drugged her when she came by to see me." What Tyler didn't know was that his brother raped her also. That was the next photo Al showed him.

Al asked, "Haven't you seen these pictures before?"

"Just some of them on the computer. Brian sends them to us by email."

"Guess your buddy Brian screwed you too. How old is your best friend's sister?"

"Seventeen."

"So, you kinda thought of her as a girlfriend?"

Tyler was hurt, angry and felt powerless. He put his hands on his face and nodded.

Al knew the recorder didn't hear head nods. "So, you're nodding your head, does that mean you wanted her to be your girlfriend?"

"Yes."

Al turned to a picture of another victim that he'd marked because all three guys had pictures of themselves raping her, "What about this girl, how long ago was this?"

"Three months ago, I think."

"Did you screw her when she was passed out?"

"Ya."

"Where did you find her?" Al had to nail down a few solid victims that already had been IDed, because cases like these were made by giving the jury full stories on three or four victims, not by generalities of dozens of victims.

"Brian, he brought her home."

"So, did he screw her also?"

"Ya."

"Did Bradley?"

"Ya."

"So, did she ever figure out what happened to her?"

"Not as far as I know."

The flood gates were open. Tyler was angry and wanted revenge on Brian Defoe for raping his girlfriend and he didn't care if it hurt him or his brother to get his revenge done. He would later, but by then it would be too late. Al would have them all recorded. He had Tyler confessing to the two major elements of rape--lack of consent and intercourse--with photographic evidence to support the confession. He had statements on four different victims and plenty of verifiable facts to support the statements.

When Al called in the other two suspects, one at a time, he basically duplicated his tactics with them. He did add one little element. "Before you give your statement, I want you to hear what Tyler had to say." He then played Tyler's confession before he said, "Now, I know you don't want to be a certified liar, so why don't you explain your perspective on these pictures." Both suspects realized denial was pointless and blamed the other one, saying it was their idea and they'd just gone along with it.

After four and a half hours of interrogation Al was exhausted but walked away satisfied. He'd cracked a tough nut and had the key to sending three predators away for long prison sentences. As Al was securing the recordings for transcription, he couldn't help but wonder what part internet porn and online anonymity played in teaching these boneheads to be criminals.

DOJ and detective division would eventually identify 96 of the suspected 134 victims. The painstaking case required that the investigators show bar employees and patrons of the three target bars headshot photos of the victims and ask if they knew them. The investigators found that some of the underage victims were drugged at house parties populated by high school and community college students. The victim's reaction to the police explanation of the case was across the spectrum. Some thought something happened, but weren't sure. Others didn't believe it. Some said they knew something happened, but couldn't prove it.

The suspects were charged with rape, oral copulation and child molestation because of the underaged girls. Brian Defoe and Bradley Pope pled not guilty and after three weeks in the county jail were released on bond. Their parents put up their homes as collateral for the bail.

Tyler Pope only lasted one week in jail. He committed suicide by hanging himself with his own pants. He'd ripped them into strips and braided them to make a short rope. He tied the rope to the top bunk of a bed and raised his feet till he passed out, eventually dying from lack of oxygen. His guilt over the rape of his fantasy girlfriend and fear of decades in prison was too much for him to handle. It would complicate the case. He wouldn't be there to testify at trial and the sleaziest defense attorney in the area had already started to make motions to suppress the confessions claiming that Tyler's statement was made under threat of prison and the subsequent confessions were fruit of the poisonous tree. The defense attorney knew that the victims wouldn't want to have the photos used in court and that their lack of any clear memory was a wedge of reasonable doubt he could drive between the jury and conviction.

∞

Al, being newly divorced again, was having a cold bottle of water with Anna at her apartment two days after Tyler's death. They had gone running together, mostly as a stress reduction exercise.

As they sat on the patio cooling down Al said, "Being a crack interrogator has its down side. You get to feel responsible for a stupid shit's death."

"He was a rapist, Al. Our arrest saved dozens of potential victims."

"He was a 19-year-old stupid shit that got sucked into being a criminal by an equally stupid older brother." Al added, "I know what the job requires. I just get a belly full of idiots and fools destroying themselves and everything they touch."

Anna put her stocking feet up on Al's lap and said, "Rub those, will ya?" Al started to massage her feet.

"Al, do you know what I do when police work starts to get me down?"

Al gave Anna a smug look, "No Anna, what? Get a foot massage?"

"I watch Andy Griffith reruns about police work in Mayberry and drink chocolate milk. Want some?"

"Sure, why not."

CHAPTER 14

Cam really needed to get coordinated on this parolee stakeout project, but Erin's roofie rapist case had sucked up everyone's time lately. All the narcs he needed to chase down parolees were conducting interviews and chasing the loose ends of that investigation. Several of his people were trying to nail down the source of the rohypnol, which was a long shot at best. On top of that, they had their normal informant buys and search warrants to serve. Lieutenant Glen thought all this was fine, except that he was losing supervisors, Cam and Erin, one day a week to patrol and he'd wanted to remedy that.

Cam and Erin were summoned to a conference in Glen's office.

Glen was grazing on a gourmet snack that his girlfriend Carol had made for him when the two Sergeants arrived. "Sit down and give me a report on what you two hot shots have been up to."

Cam gave an open hand gesture to Erin to go first.

"Well, Lieutenant, I've about wrapped up the 261 case. The county people are still conducting interviews of the rape victims, but the DA says he has enough to proceed in court. IDing victims at this point, is more of a should-do thing than a needed-to-do thing. We're not having much luck tracing the rohypnol source. I suspect it was a connection Defoe made several years ago. Tyler Pope told Al before he hung himself, that the Pope brothers got their dope from Defoe."

Glen nodded and looked at Cam.

Cam said, "I've been surveilling parolees with what manpower Erin has left me and trying to do our normal thing. I've got a few good buy cases coming to a head."

Erin frowned at Cam, "Poor baby."

Glen nodded again and asked Cam, "You have anything planned this week that could irritate patrol?"

Cam gave Glen a quizzical look, "What?"

Glen explained, "Patrol is getting too comfortable with this Sergeant sharing and I need to remind them of why they shouldn't steal my people. Erin's roofie case made them ecstatic about the crossover and I don't want them to think of this thing as a permanent assignment."

Cam offered, "I could do another DUI check point and offer a little twist that Randy came up with. It's guaranteed to get their attention."

Glen quickly added, "I don't want to know about any patrol related activities you have planned. That's none of my business, but when you've completed it, I'd love to hear all about it." He was suppressing a smile.

He stood up, signaling that the meeting was over. "Oh Erin, keep your ears open. I'm catching some rumors about one of your rape victims being related to a retired cop I know."

"Will do, Lieutenant."

∞

Cam walked into the narc squad room and saw Jesse typing away on his computer. "Hey Kahuna, you got a minute?"

"Sure Sarge, I'm just finishing up my Christmas list for Santa: one inflatable wahine, one Sergeant disintegrator gun, a surf board with a beer cooler rear seat."

"You're a funny man, Jesse Hale, I'm glad you're in the mood for levity because I've got a job that requires a sense of humor."

Jesse had a slightly worried look on his face because Cam was known to hang it out there once and a while.

"Here's the deal, Jesse. We're gonna do another DUI check point with dogs and narcs this Friday and Saturday, but we're going to add Randy's little Drug Checkpoint feature."

Jesse looked at Cam and tilted his head to the side. "You've been hit in the head too many times doing that karate stuff of yours."

"Probably true, but I was encouraged by higher ups, so pay attention. We need it set up just like before, but I want two more staging areas without DUI officers. On these you're going to put out a sign that says, Drug Checkpoint Inspection Area."

Jesse said, "What?"

"That's right, now there won't be a checkpoint because that would be illegal, but you will have a few marked traffic units to follow and stop anyone who spins an illegal U-turn. That's where you come in. You have to set these up in areas where the driver either lawfully drives forward or illegally turns around, which gives us the probable cause to stop them. We'll have a K-9 unit to assist with the stop."

Jesse grinned, "Oh, that's diabolical. Randy's gonna love this. It really is the old pretext stop justification. They could drive right on as normal or by making an illegal turn give us probable cause to stop them and it incriminates them. I love it."

"Okay Jesse, this is your monkey, make it happen."

"10-4 boss. Randy! Front and center, you bomb-throwing nut job."

Jesse and Randy huddled at Jesse's desk and began to plot their attack.

CHAPTER 15

Juan Ortiz was tying up a few loose ends of his own. He needed some cold guns and two hot cars for the grocery store robbery he had planned. The gang had guns, but he needed some that weren't traceable back to any gang member. The weapons he possessed now had been used in a few drive-bys and would point a finger in the gang's direction. Juan wanted the cops to think this was a random group of armed robbers rather than a gang robbery.

He knew a guy who bought guns under other people's names and resold them. It always helps to know a "straw buyer." Juan decided that they would steal the two cars they needed for the robbery the morning of the rip off. If they stole them too much in advance the cops might be looking for them already. He decided that before he went to purchase the guns, he'd take everybody through a dry run of the robbery. They wouldn't do anything suspicious, but the stick-up team of four people would walk through the grocery store so they could get a good lay of the land. They would park two cars outside the two exits, so that either one could be used to escape. The cars they used for the mock robbery wouldn't be hot and they wouldn't phone in a false diversion call across town, but everything else would be the same. Juan's rehearsal was so realistic that it scared the crap out of Bobby and Tommy.

Bobby and Tommy were trying to figure out how a group of homeless people were getting their meth. These folks would hang out in a city park right across the street from a senior citizen housing complex. Many of these elderly citizens rented in this building because it had a nice park and a major grocery store nearby. It allowed them a place to walk and sit outside, weather permitting. The grocery store was so close by that the seniors could push their shopping basket to the apartment building for later collection by the store. All that changed when the drug addicts decided that the park was theirs. The old people were frightened of the users, so they gave them money when the panhandlers asked. They were afraid not to, even though they were told it was perpetuating the problem. The grocery store found that the meth heads were chasing off good citizens other than the seniors, so they moved the store to a site a half mile away. That eliminated the drug users, but also made it impossible to use for the older apartment dwellers who didn't have transportation. The result was the elderly tenants would have neither a grocery store nor a park to use and were imprisoned in their own apartments. This was a perfect formula for urban blight.

Bobby wanted to do something about this, but getting rid of drug addicts was a lot like chasing away sea gulls at the beach. He and Tommy thought a good way to start was to surveil some of the homeless addicts and see where they were scoring their dope.

As Tommy was driving into the old grocery store parking lot, he noticed the bicyclist they were following was riding a nicer than normal street bike. He looked to be in his 30's and wasn't your typical homeless drug addict. That's why they followed him. It wasn't until they saw two different drug addicts look behind some pallets sitting beside the store that they figured out what was occurring. The addict would go behind the pallets and drop off some money, then the dealer would ride his bike over and look in the same spot. He'd pick up the money and drop off the dope. He even had a large bag of aluminum cans for recycling to look the part.

A community group had sponsored a website to fund cell phones for the homeless so they could stay in touch, which helped dealers and users stay in touch. No good deed goes unpunished.

Bobby and Tommy watched this all go down a couple of times and talked about a strategy for handling the dope sales.

Tommy said, "if we jump out and arrest him now, we won't be able to prove sales. He might not be holding enough dope."

"Ya, that's a problem. I think we should just watch him and document what he's doing. ID him somehow and get a warrant for him and his house if we can. Maybe we could hit him when he leaves home to deal. Then he'll be holding big."

Tommy added, "I bet he has a real house and this is all just a front. Push comes to shove we can get a marked unit to ID him for some minor bull like a bike license or panhandling complaint."

"Sounds good."

As they sat back and watched they started to notice what looked suspiciously like a robbery or someone casing the place for a robbery.

Juan Ortiz pulled his car up in front of the Safeway store's North entrance with another Hispanic male in the vehicle. At the same time another car pulled up in front of the South entrance with two Hispanic males. All four of these guys looked like hard-core gang members.

Bobby looked at Tommy, "Partner, that's Juan Ortiz and it's not just a coincidence that he's with three other tatted up Mexicans entering the store from two different doors."

"Ya, but look at their clothes. I don't see guns or bulky clothes that could cover guns and they aren't covered up to hide their faces."

Bobby thought about what Tommy said, "Right, this doesn't make sense unless it's a dry run to get a feel for a robbery. We know from Danny Dominguez that Ortiz is a 211 man who's likely to do it again, but I'm with you, it doesn't look like it's going down right now. Let's just watch and see what happens."

Tommy asked, "How bout I just stroll into the store and buy something? They don't know me and maybe I'll get a few details we'd miss out here."

Bobby, being a Corporal and in charge said, "Okay, but don't burn yourself and if a robbery goes down, don't do anything but be a good witness. You're in plain clothes with a few tats of your own and the uniformed cops will shoot you."

"10-4."

Tommy slid out of the undercover vehicle and went inside. Bobby wrote down both plate numbers and started using his radio to search for other narcs nearby that could help with a surveillance. He wasn't having much luck. Todd and Randy were across town and their response time was too long to be helpful. Terence happened to be working traffic that day and overheard the radio traffic. He got on the air because he recognized Bobby's voice, and asked if he could be of any assistance.

"Affirmative, 1-Adam 17. 11-98 the Exxon station across from the Safeway."

About 5 minutes later Bobby saw Terrence arrive across the street. He told him to stand by for a minute because he noticed Ortiz and his friends all exit the store using two different exits. They walked calmly to their cars and a few seconds later Tommy walked out of the store and walked slowly toward Bobby. Tommy shook his head sideways to indicate that nothing went down. Bobby breathed a sigh of relief. He really didn't want to handle a robbery in plain clothes with no planning or backup.

Tommy opened the car door and said, "Find anybody to help follow these guys?"

Bobby said, "Just Terrence in a marked unit which won't help much. I think I'll have him ID the dope dealer on the bicycle and we'll follow Ortiz."

Bobby handed Tommy the radio and said, "Explain to Terrence what we want him to do."

"1 Adam 17, 10-6 to channel 4." Now that Tommy had Terrence on a radio channel that wasn't used much, he could explain what he needed.

"Hey Terrence, it's Tommy."

"What are you narcs doing on my beat? Nothing crazy I hope."

"Nah, we just need you to ID that guy riding the bicycle North on 14th. He's a dope dealer and we need to know who he is and where he lives without spooking him. We want to hit him with a warrant later on. Do some of that razzle dazzle vehicle code stuff you do and find out his particulars. Bobby and I need to follow a couple of guys that could be casing the store for a 211."

Terrence said, "10-4, and let me know about this 211 investigation. I hate surprises."

Tommy said, "You bet, and thanks."

CHAPTER 16

Jesse and Randy decided that it wasn't necessary to start from scratch. They already had a successful plan for a DUI checkpoint with dogs added to sniff out dope and guns, so they just duplicated their previous two DUI checkpoints in a new location. Jesse was an equal opportunity narc and believed rich people deserved as much police service as poor citizens, so he set up the DUI checkpoint in upper-class neighborhoods. It worked just as well as the last time because rich people drive drunk and use dope just like poor folk. The difference is they whine about getting caught a lot more.

The new tactic that Cam was implementing by setting up a drug checkpoint sign on a street that didn't lawfully allow U-turns was breaking new legal ground. They picked two areas that had light traffic and were frequently used to get to another city. A big sign was posted under lights that said, "Drug Checkpoint-Proceed into the Cones." Far ahead on the roadway the narcs had directed the traffic into a lane outlined by traffic cones and then redirected the traffic back on to the roadway without ever stopping them. The results were comical. Most people slowed and drove through the cones only to find nothing stopping them from driving back into their traffic lane and proceeding on their way. Some stopped and pulled to the side of the road. A few, emptied contraband out the car window, which was observed by narcs parked behind them using field glasses. These folks were stopped by marked units with a narc back-up and charged with littering on a public roadway and possession of whatever drug was found. In some cases, the littering ticket would be a more severe punishment than the dope. Others made a U-turn right in the middle of the highway, which was illegal. They would be stopped by a traffic unit and a narc car equipped with a dope dog. The narcs and traffic officers pulled this operation two nights in a row at the same location. They thought initially that the second night wouldn't be as productive because the word would go out, but they were wrong. They arrested just as many people at both the DUI checkpoints and the Drug checkpoints.

Cam was talking with Jesse at the scene of one of the Drug checkpoints standing back from a surveillance station where they were monitoring citizens with field glasses.

"You know, Cam, come Monday morning there will be a line of citizens and defense attorneys at the complaint counter sniveling about the unfair tactics they were subjected to."

"Ya, I suspect you're right. We can't please all our customers."

Just as Jesse was about to ask Cam a question, one of the traffic units that was attempting to pull over a U-turn violator called in a pursuit. In police work there are two closely related calls: "Failure to Yield" and "In Pursuit." The difference is subtle but legally important. Failure to yield means the citizen just didn't stop for you. They're required to pull over, but some people just keep driving. In pursuit means they see your red lights and stomp on the gas because they want to lose you.

Jesse got on the air with the traffic unit and asked, "2-Bravo 23, I thought you had a Failure to Yield?"

"Affirmative N18, it was for two miles, but now they're running."

Another traffic unit got on the air, "2-Bravo 23, 2-Bravo 29, I'm right behind you."

Jesse ordered all the other units to back off. Two officers tailing this pursuit were enough. He waited. Cam sat his portable on the roof of his car and listened to the cars pursuing the U-turn vehicle and waited also. Jesse gave him a shrug as if to say, "Who knows?"

"Jesse, I think it's about time to wind this up. We've made 17 arrests in two nights. That ought to be enough to get everybody excited and we're dipping into Lieutenant Glen's overtime budget significantly."

"No doubt about that. I'll talk with the troops." Jesse got in his car to tell the other officers to wrap it up. Just a few minutes later as Cam sat in his car, he received a radio call.

"N6, 2-Bravo 23."

"N6.'

"10-11 at our stop. This situation requires a zebra (someone with stripes on their arm)."

Cam rolled up behind the two marked units and saw that they had a female cuffed in the rear of marked unit. She was in her 60's and dressed in a suit with pearls and a hat.

Cam smiled at his two officers, "On her way to the senior prom?"

23 said, "Gets crazy, Sarg. She's been drinking, loaded on Ambien and has two other prescriptions in her possession that are not hers. She's stoned out of her gourd, but it looks like a lab's going to have to sort out, on what."

Cam said, "Ya, okay, why did you need me?"

23 smiled and said, "Oh yeah, she's a councilman's wife, a lawyer and she pissed. She really does not like your check point idea."

Cam dropped his head forward, then raised it smiling. "Do real good reports guys, because everybody will be quoting them. I'll send a couple of my narcs to help with the dope part of the investigation." Cam was absolutely sure this would get the attention Lieutenant Glen was looking for. If this "Operation Check Point," didn't get him fired, it just might get him booted out of patrol.

∞

Cam wasn't the only one having patrol do narcotics work. Bobby was holding up his end by having Terrence identify the bicycle rider who was dealing meth to all the homeless people. Terrence stopped Edwin Roberts with a flash of red lights and a short blast of his horn.

When Terrence wanted to be creative, he excelled. He pulled his radio mic off of the hanging clip and looped the cord over his rearview mirror, allowing it to dangle in the wind. He found a tooth pick in his duty bag and stuck it into his mouth. To finish off the redneck image he stuck both thumbs in the front of his gun belt and ambled toward the drug dealer. He looked like a character out of a Southern police drama.

"Well now, partner, you seem to think them red lights are for everybody but you. Bicycles got to obey the law too, ya know."

The bike riding crank dealer was nervous, but thought this stupid old redneck cop probably wouldn't shake him down for dope.

"Sorry, officer, guess my mind was somewhere else. Did I ride through that light?"

"I'm guessing ya, son. Break out some ID for me. Who are you? You got that bike licensed?"

Edwin Roberts dug around in his pocket and came out with a wallet. He found a driver's license that was current and handed it to Terrence. Terrence acted like he was a sloppy cop, but was watching every move this guy made. He looked for bulges near his waist band and analyzed his behavior. The crook was supposed to be a homeless guy collecting cans, but he had a current license to drive. Why the bike? He also was stone sober. A meth dealer that didn't use was a cut above as a businessman. He also was too clean and well-fed.

"You live at this address, Mr. Roberts?"

"Yes officer."

"You got any warrants out for you?"

"No, I'm clear."

"I'll be the judge of that." Terrence keyed the mic on his portable and ran Edwin. As he was waiting for the records search to return, he asked Edwin several harmless questions. When dispatch hit him on the radio, Terrence stepped away from the suspect.

"1-Adam 17, your subject is clear."

"10-4, burn a copy for my box, would you?"

Dispatch said, "Copy." Now Terrence had all the information on the suspect to forward to Tommy and Bobby.

"Okay partner, you're clear. You ride that bicycle with a little more attention to the law, ya hear?"

Edwin Roberts was breathing a sigh of relief. This stupid cop was letting him ride away with six hits of meth all wrapped separately and ready for sale. "I will officer, thanks." He pedaled away laughing inside.

∞

Bobby and Tommy thought it was awfully nice of Juan Ortiz and the other carload of crooks to make life easy for them. They both drove slowly and directly to a gang house located across town. After they parked and went inside Bobby told Tommy to grab the field glasses and get all the license plate numbers parked at the home. They would have to run these guys through DMV and then through records to see what they could find. Danny Dominguez would also be a good source of information.

Cam listened intently as Bobby ran down the information about Juan Ortiz and his mock robbery run. Danny Dominguez listened even more intently.

Danny said, "The cars that were parked in front of the gang house were a wealth of information. The registered owners were all gang members of the Nortenos and Ortiz is expressly forbidden from associating with them as a condition of his parole. I can wrap him up right now and send him back to the joint."

Cam nodded his head and proceeded carefully, "Danny, how long would you be able to extend his sentence with this parole violation?"

"Well, six months anyway."

Cam smiled, "And then what?"

Danny gave Cam a questioning look, "What do you mean?"

"I guess I mean, when Ortiz gets out after six months, what will he do?"

Danny got it, "Ya, another robbery."

"Right. Let's allow this thing to go down and wrap him and his buddies up just like a Christmas package."

Danny Dominguez didn't like this plan. It violated everything parole was about. He was supposed to stop crime when his people were going to be involved. "What if someone gets hurt?"

Bobby thought it was time to talk because he didn't want Danny and Cam to get into an entrenched debate. "We know that civilian injuries are a real concern. The problem we have is if we never allow the crimes to happen then we're stuck with attempted crimes. They're hard to prove in court and never have a decent sentence attached. There are things we can do to mitigate civilian risk and I'll make sure we're careful with this one since Ortiz is such a gunslinger."

Danny wasn't completely convinced, but he also didn't have enough evidence of a pending crime to violate Ortiz's parole. All he really had was Bobby's observations, which would never be proof in court.

"Okay Cam, we'll do it your way even though I have my doubts. Maybe it's just as well if you leave me out of any of your reports. I'm thinking my superiors wouldn't like this at all."

"Sure Danny, we'll keep you updated, but it'll be unofficially. Make sure you don't change your supervision routine with Ortiz because we don't want him to get suspicious."

"Right," Danny picked up his coffee and before he left, he said, "Cam, he won't go peacefully and he's smarter than he seems. Watch yourself."

Cam and Bobby nodded.

CHAPTER 17

Captain Johnson summoned Lieutenants Glen and Bledsoe to his office. They both knew that it wasn't for a tea social. If they both were to attend then it was obvious that it was regarding something they had in common, like Sergeants they shared.

"Gentlemen, someone detonated a shit bomb in the Chief's office." The Lieutenants waited. "Which one of you would like to explain who's responsible for this chain of events?"

Bledsoe and Glen looked at each other for a moment, then Glen smiled and looked at the Captain. "Well, Captain, I guess you could call this a combined operation. Our hybrid Sergeants used both patrol and narcotics officers to execute this somewhat creative operation. While I understand the Chief's problem, I don't apologize for the actions of my officers. The tactics were unusual, but effective. The arrests and seizures were impressive. It appears as though their main mistake was enforcing the law on rich connected people instead of the usual poor folk."

Captain Johnson could see where Glen's head was at, so he looked at Lieutenant Bledsoe for his perspective.

"While I agree with Bud, this was a bit of a surprise. These narcs do shit first and explain it later, but I don't fault their tactics. The case law, I believe, will support this and the complaints have more to do with tactics than guilt. All these people who got busted were breaking the law, their sniveling was about how they got caught. To quote my friend Bud, this is defense attorney logic."

Captain Johnson said, "So, neither one of you authorized this caper, but neither of you have a problem with it. Is that right?"

Both Glen and Bledsoe shrugged and nodded slightly.

Johnson was irritated. "You know, if neither of you are supervising these people then no one is."

Glen and Bledsoe didn't quite know how to respond, but eventually Glen spoke up. "This would appear to be the problem with a split supervision situation. I remember a dog that a girlfriend and I shared a while back. The poor bastard either got fed four times a day or went hungry."

Captain Johnson tilted back in his highbacked chair and rubbed his head with an open palm. "Okay gentleman, how about both of you issue orders to stand down on any more of these DUI stops with dogs and checkpoint detours till the smoke clears. If it was just mad defense attorneys we had to deal with that would be one thing, but busting the councilman's wife added a whole new dimension to this operation."

Both Glen and Bledsoe stood up and nodded as they moved to the door. They walked silently through a set of double doors leaving the administrative wing of the building and when the doors shut Bledsoe let out a laugh he'd been holding in as he half doubled over.

He playful punched Glen in the shoulder and said, "I almost feel sorry for that poor bastard."

Glen let out a chuckle, "You want to guess how long it will be before I get my Sergeants back?"

"I'm guessing very soon, but God damn it Bud, you got to help me with this Sergeant thing. The lack of supervision is killing me."

Bud nodded, "Ya, we'll give it some thought." He slapped Bledsoe on the shoulder as he walked back to the narc squad room. He wished he saw as much humor in the situation as Bledsoe did. He had a bad feeling about this problem.

∞

Glen called Cam, Erin, Bobby and Jesse in to his office for a meeting the next day. He gave them the short version of his meeting with Lieutenant Bledsoe and Captain Johnson.

"So, it looks like we take a break from the DUI and Check Point operation for a few weeks. I'm sure Bledsoe will talk with you two on your patrol shift. It's just as well, since we need to see how the case law shakes out on the arrests anyway. Also, I told Bledsoe that we'd think about some solution to his supervision shortage since I'm guessing you guys have spoiled that party. I'm not quite sure what it would be, but give it some thought."

Erin didn't need to think about it, "Terrence." Glen and the guys all looked at her. "That hard-headed mule has been resisting promotion for years and I think if we all ganged up on him, he'd cave. He's been acting supervisor so often he wouldn't even notice the change."

Bobby added, "Except in his paycheck."

Jesse rubbed his chin with the back of his fingers, "Maybe Erin needs to talk with Josephine. Go for the wife, the soft underbelly of this problem."

Glen laughed as he stood up and pointed at Erin in agreement.

CHAPTER 18

Cynthia Spencer was getting the administrative run around and in her raw emotional condition government was becoming the enemy. She had rights and if they weren't going to cooperate, she'd have her attorney hammer them.

She sat across the desk from Erin and said, "I know my rights. My dad was a cop. I want to see all the pictures you have of me." She was referring to the rape pictures taken by Defoe and the Pope brothers. The officers attempting to identify the victims made headshots of her to show bar employees and patrons. The investigators later gave her a general idea of the nature of the rape pictures, but never showed them to her. She had asked but was told that only the District Attorney could authorize that.

Erin asked, "Have you talked with the DA?"

"Yes, and they gave me the run around. I couldn't get a straight answer, just a 'we'll process your request.' If this were you, wouldn't you want to know what happened to you?"

Erin paused for a few seconds, "This whole thing could be very traumatic for you. I guess I'd want to know, but I don't think I'd ever advise anybody to go down that road."

Cynthia stared at Erin, "I'm not backing off of this."

Erin nodded, "Okay, let me talk with the Deputy DA that's handling this and I'll call you back. I'll try to get authorization."

Cynthia stood up, "Thank you. How soon?"

"A day or two."

After Cynthia left the office Erin phoned Lieutenant Glen. She explained the request and the problem.

"She'll see them at trial time. She's one of the cases they plan to present, so she'll be asked to verify her identity in the photos on the witness stand. I can't believe that will be the first time she sees them. The DA would be nuts to allow that emotional explosion to happen without warning."

Erin knew Glen was right, "So, what do you recommend?"

"Call the DA and get permission, then get ready. It'll be ugly." Erin wasn't quite sure why Glen didn't hand this off to the task force or DA, but that was his prerogative. Maybe it was because of the law enforcement connection.

The Deputy DA relented. He agreed that any decent attorney could get the photos and confessed the only reason he didn't do it before now was because it would be such an emotional scene that he didn't want to go there till he had to. The prosecution was weeks off and he was hoping for a guilty plea. Erin called Cynthia Spencer back and set up a date for her to view the photos. She asked Cynthia to please bring a family member or friend to accompany her. Erin would also have an advocate from the women's crisis shelter on hand.

Betty Ward from the crisis shelter was a gifted psychologist who volunteered at the shelter as needed. She was a large, confident woman in her 60's who made clients believe she was their mother. Erin had used her services before and knew from past experiences that she respected cops and wanted to help rather than find fault. Betty had been briefed by Erin on the case and specifically on Cynthia's involvement.

Betty arrived 15 minutes early and as usual was a step ahead of everybody. "You handling this okay Erin?"

Erin smiled at her, "Just another day in paradise."

"Wishing you could just take that gun of yours and clean up this little problem without all the fuss?"

"Betty, I recommend you buy a lottery ticket on the way home. You're clairvoyant today."

∞

Cynthia Spencer walked into Erin's office with her older sister. Both Betty and Erin were glad to see her choice. They knew that at some point they had to send her home and were relieved that someone would be there to look after her. Erin introduced Betty and explained that it was standard police procedure to have an advocate present. They seemed to accept that without a problem. The three women sat facing Erin in office chairs. Erin explained what the photos had portrayed as a way of softening the blow, then she handed them to Cynthia. As she peeled off eight different full paged pictures of her nude, being raped by three different men and close-up genital photos she started to shake and cry uncontrollable. Erin gathered up the photos and slid them into her desk drawer. Her sister scooted her chair next to Cynthia's and held her hand. She didn't seem to know what to say.

Betty waited for what Erin thought was a long time. She got out of her chair and walked up to Cynthia. She said, "Stand up, dear. Stand up." She reached forward and helped Cynthia to stand, then she wrapped her arms around her and held her tight in a big hug, to show her she wasn't untouchable. "They used your body, they did not use your mind. You are a strong, independent woman and you'll get through this. We'll put these bastards in jail and you'll go on with your life. Don't let them win by letting them control your emotions. I know you feel powerless and afraid, but we're all here to help you. Don't let this one crime define who you are."

Cynthia cried some more and seemed to melt into Betty's chest. Erin stood up and made eye contact with Betty as she walked toward the door. Betty nodded as Erin exited. Betty looked at the older sister who wasn't sure what to do and said, "You can stay here with us while we talk. It will be helpful to have you remind her of what we discussed. Now honey, tell me what thoughts are crashing around in your head right now."

Erin walked down the hall to get some coffee. She saw Jesse reading some reports in front of the copy machine and walked up in front of him and hugged him. He was a little surprised and hugged her back without talking. She walked on to get her coffee.

Chapter 19

Juan Ortiz was happy with the dry run at the grocery store. He'd dreamed about this robbery and had every detail worked out in his head. He wouldn't make any of the same mistakes he'd made last time. In order to keep the cops away from the store he planned to have two gang members start a fire across town near a convalescent hospital. Then they'd phone in a fake call telling the cops that the patients were in danger. That would get the cops out of the way for a few minutes. Juan also planned to use two getaway cars, so the four robbers could pick either one depending on which one was the closest. The keys would be left under the driver's floor mat. He planned to only drive them a short way before he switched to vehicles that weren't stolen. He had it all covered and the timing was set. The only thing left to do was get some cold guns that couldn't be traced back to the gang.

∞

Bobby told Cam that they had a ton of stuff going down and needed some coordination, so Cam needed to set up a meeting with all the supervisors.

Cam called Glen to see if he wanted to attend, but was told by the Lieutenant to "handle it," because he was out of town for a few days. Glen said, "have someone take notes and forward them to me." Cam thought this smelled like Glen was testing him.

When Cam had all the Sergeants and Corporals present, he said, "Bobby why don't you start? Lay out all the cases we have and your ideas. I'll take some notes for Lieutenant Glen."

"Okay, well we've got several competing issues. First, and probably most important, our friend Juan Ortiz looks ready to pull a 211 at the Safeway. He's cased the place and the latest regurgitation of the computer program says in will go down over the three-day weekend. That's when they'll have a bunch of money on hand and Ortiz is a grandiose crook and wants to think of himself as a mastermind criminal according to his PO Danny. We've got to think about how to cover that."

"Then there's the meth dealer that Terrence IDed for us. This guy has a few priors and looks to be a serious source of dope, especially for street people. He's making the senior citizen park a virtual zombie land all by himself.

"And then there's Erin's roofie rapist case. It's slopping over into a few other areas. All the victims are demanding disclosure because one of them has taken to the internet and posted all their theories, desires, rights and information on the suspects. This promises to be a vigilantly nightmare."

"Meanwhile, back at the ranch, you've got a City Councilman and his lawyer wife dissecting your DUI and Drug Check Point cases."

"I think that about covers it."

Cam covered his head with both arms, "Well, shit! When you put it like that, I'm a little depressed." Everyone laughed. "Okay, first thing first. Ortiz is our priority. Ideas?"

Erin said, "We have to have a solid surveillance on him starting before the three-day weekend with some of our guys pulling overtime."

Cam asked, "Jesse, how's the upgraded weapon certification coming?"

"Both Todd and I are cleared to use the M4 assault rifles. SWAT will be available, but realistically they'll take too long to get there because we don't know exactly when it's going down. This thing will happen fast and we really don't want a rolling gun battle, so we should handle it in the parking lot."

Bobby added, "We should think about having some people walking the perimeter of the store entrances to move civilians out of the way."

Everyone waited for Cam to digest all this information. "Alright Jesse, you and Bobby set up a tactical plan to cover the parking lot. That should include neutralizing their vehicles, an ambush site to arrest them, civilian safety and anything else you can think of. Make sure you include notifying other agencies and especially our patrol division, so undercover cops don't get shot by uniforms. I want it to be detailed; weapons, vehicles, body armor, the works."

Cam made a few notes then looked at Bobby, "Could we dump this meth dealer on Tommy and Terrence?

Bobby said, "I guess, but Terrence doesn't work for the narc squad. He's a patrol officer."

Cam nodded, "Ya, but that distinction has been blurred lately and he was involved with the IDing of the suspect. You're gonna be busy with this Ortiz 211 and it would be good training for both Tommy and Terrence. I might even make Terrence want to be a Sergeant, so he doesn't get dragged into all these crazy narc capers." Everyone laughed.

"Erin, what ideas do you have about this 261 case?"

She paused a moment, "Bobby's right, this thing has developed a life of its own. I've started to get calls from victims, people who think they're victims with no evidence to support the claim, attorneys and nuts from A to Z. I am worried about vigilante behavior because one of the online activists has posted very specific data about the two surviving suspects."

Jesse asked, "What's the DA's position on all this?"

Erin nodded. "Well, I've kinda dumped the whole thing in their lap. I decided that I can't deal with all the volume of victim requests, so I've just been referring the calls from victims to them. They've set up a contact person to deal specifically with this case. Betty Ward the shrink, is working with them. Our detective division's tech expert is trying to track some of the online threats. No telling if they're credible. Oh, I almost forgot, Lieutenant Glen mentioned that one of the victims was a cop's kid and Cynthia Spencer mentioned to me in passing at our first meeting that her dad was a cop. I just found out that he's made a few demands of the DA's office and the Deputy DA handling this thing thinks he's a powder keg ready to blow. Glen wanted to be informed because he knows the guy."

The other guys in the meeting just shook their heads. Cam said, "I don't see what we can do at this point except hand things off to the DA. If we step on their toes, it could affect the prosecution. Once the legal process is started, we really have to coordinate through them."

Erin answered, "Right, that's my opinion also. Oh, one other thing. Santa Clara County sexual assault investigation unit ran some scans on our victims and believes that some of the pictures were posted on a revenge porn site. They're still working on that piece of the investigation."

Cam said sarcastically, "Swell."

CHAPTER 20

Tommy cranked out a search warrant using all the information and observations he and Bobby got by investigating Edwin Roberts, the bicycle meth dealer. Terrence's attached statement was signed under penalty of perjury. An on-call judge read the warrant with a skeptical look on his face as Tommy waited.

"Detective Aquilar, this is a well-written search warrant except for one critical component. You don't actually have any meth, nor do you prove in any way that there was any meth exchanged." He handed it back to Tommy, "Try again son, when you have some linkage established."

Tommy went back to the squad room and passed Bobby sitting at a desk.

"How did it go Tommy?"

Tommy didn't make eye contact with Bobby as he walked by, "I'm still working on it." He saw Todd returning from lunch. "Hey, doing anything?"

Todd said, "Na, bullshit paperwork."

"Come with me. I need help." Tommy explained his problem with the warrant and his idea about how to fix it. He was pissed. This was a show of confidence that the Sergeants had him chase down this warrant and he'd fucked it up by not tying the dealer to some meth. He'd fix that. "Okay Todd, let's find this dirt bag."

Todd and Tommy went to the areas where they observed the suspect dealing previously and within an hour, he pedaled his bike behind a shopping center. Through field glasses they saw him get off his bike and place something in some tall grass at the edge of a planter. There had been a homeless woman setting there briefly, when they arrived. The dealer pedaled away and the women returned.

After she started to walk away Todd said, "Let's do it before she snorts it all. Your crook's out of sight." Tommy angled the car in front of her as Todd jumped out. "Police, put your hands on your head!" Todd grabbed both her arms by her sweat shirt sleeves and placed them on her head.

Tommy stepped around in front of her and said, "We're not going to hurt you. Just relax and tell us where the dope is." She looked around licking her lips and didn't say a word. Tommy went to the first obvious location and patted down the front pocket of the sweat shirt. He felt the plastic bag inside and then removed it. The woman tried to take it back but Todd held her arms up in the air.

Todd said, "No, you can't have it, it's evidence now. Put your hands behind your back." Todd eased her hands down and cuffed her, then he sat her in the back seat of their car so she wouldn't run away. "Tommy why don't you call for transport and tell them we need a female searched." He added, "If she uses her cell to contact our dealer it might blow your whole plan." Tommy had all her property piled on the hood of their car. He cracked open her phone and pulled out the sim card. He resealed the phone and slipped the card into a deep side pocket of her backpack amongst paper and junk like only a tweaker can collect.

After they had her in the marked unit Tommy said, "I'd really like to have one more of these to convince that fussy judge. The trick is to do it so the suspect doesn't get spooked. The broken phone should buy us some time with her."

Todd motioned toward the car, "He pedaled South toward the little park in that housing development." Tommy jumped into the driver's seat. As Tommy slowly drove around the park, he was getting discouraged. He didn't see the dealer.

Todd was looking through field glasses and talking to Tommy at the same time: "Could you not try to hit every damn pothole in this road? There, over by the big elm tree on the east side. He's taken off his coat and I don't see his bike, but that's him.

"How can you be sure?"

"Shoes, Tommy, it's something Bobby taught me. It's hard to switch your shoes. I remembered those expensive high tops and thought, right, every homeless guy has those. Find a park and we'll see where he drops his load."

Within ten minutes they saw him bend over and slide something under a broken piece of concrete pavement. He walked around a large bush and pedaled off on his bike which he'd hidden.

Tommy said, "So, now we wait for the pick-up guy." A young skinny male who couldn't have been sixteen lifted up the rock and walked away.

"Let's go, Tommy." As they drove parallel on the street they got about as close as they could by vehicle.

Tommy parked and said, "Todd, you go right up behind him. Herd him toward me and I'll go left and circle around in front of him."

Todd said, "10-4, road runner."

Both Todd and Tommy ran to get into their positions. Todd came out from behind a grove of trees about 50 yards from the suspect. Tommy had covered twice the ground to make sure he was in front. Todd started to close the gap by running when the suspect turned around and saw him. He bolted. Tommy was watching the whole thing from behind a tree and when the suspect broke into a run Tommy sprinted at an angle back toward him. The guy must have had a little meth still in his system and a full load of adrenaline because he moved with impressive speed. Tommy admired his effort, but it wasn't going to work. Tommy had run cross country in college and still ran to stay in shape. Once they had established a pace, Tommy stepped it up a little closing the gap. The farther they ran the slower the guy progressed. Tommy knew that grabbing a running person was messy and often hurt both people involved when they went down. He remembered how the slightest bump or foot tangle sent runners flying during a race, so he got within arm distance and hit the suspect with an open hand on the shoulder pushing him forward and sideways. The suspect tripped rolled and crashed into the base of a hedge. Tommy recognized the danger of weapons and more likely, destruction of the evidence, so he landed on his back, grabbed his arms and quickly cuffed him.

Todd ran up a few seconds later breathing hard. His weightlifter body was fast for a short sprint, but it wasn't designed for the long haul.

"Christ this guy can run. Good thing you were here. Let's see if he's holding." Todd pulled a small Ziplock of meth from the suspect's front pants pocket. They walked him over to a bench and Tommy told him to sit.

After everybody caught their breath, Tommy started the conversation, "How long you been using?"

The kid shrugged and said nothing.

"A year? Two years? Since kindergarten?"

The kid mumbled, "four months."

"So, how you using now, snort, smoke, a needle?"

"Usually snort. Sometimes with friends...you know."

Tommy nodded, "Ya, I know." Tommy really didn't care about all this background information since it wouldn't help with a warrant affidavit, but it was a way to get the kid talking. "Has the bicycle guy always been your source?"

"Well, friends in the beginning."

During this conversation Todd sat over on the end of the bench and stretched out his sore running legs. He knew that Tommy was making some progress with the kid and that his job was to stay out of the way and not threaten the guy with his size.

Tommy asked, "So, does the bike guy call you or do you call him?"

"I leave a message."

"What do you say?"

"You know... how much and when I'll be there."

"Does he have a name?"

"I don't know." Tommy knew the power of silence, so he waited. After a while the kid said, "His phone message says, 'This is Ed, leave a message'."

Tommy pulled out the kid's phone and said, "Show me his number?"

The kid told Tommy how to scroll through his phone directory and identified the dealer's number since his hands were cuffed.

"How old are you son?"

"I'll be seventeen next month."

Todd spoke for the first time since they sat down, "Sweet." He and Tommy walked the kid to their car for transport to jail and smiled at each other because this statement would seal the warrant and sales to a minor would sink this dealer.

Tommy said, "Son, I won't tell Ed you gave us information about him and I'd recommend you not talk to him about us either, because that's a good way to catch a bullet in the head. Right?"

He nodded, "Right."

Tommy called Terrence and said, "Hey, Cam says that you and I are drafting an addendum to the search warrant and planning a raid."

"Is that right? Well, I can be at the office in twenty. Will that work?"

"10-4 boss, see ya then."

CHAPTER 21

Captain Johnson knew that busting a councilman's lawyer wife was going to be a political problem, but he had no idea that the danger would come from such an unexpected angle. He thought the Drug Checkpoint issue would be hammered out in court with the DA's office dealing with the legality of the arrest. He never expected an IA complaint to be filed with the Chief regarding Cam Michaelson's conduct. And he sure never expected the complainant to be another councilman whose son was busted by the narcs and had his ear half shot off by Cam. The Chief called the Captain into his office and bypassed the Deputy Chief he was so angry. He had assigned Johnson to conduct an investigation into Cam's conduct regarding both incidents and told him to interview the councilman personally. This was the kind of career ending case that kept Captain Johnson on a steady diet of Tums and Mylanta.

Glen knew things were getting interesting when he sat down in the Captain's office because the Captain was screwing on the cap on his Mylanta bottle he'd been chugging like a beer and opened the conversation with, "I think were fucked, Bud. This is the one that will get us."

Whenever Glen heard gloom and doom statements like this, he secretly thanked his lucky stars that he was eligible to retire. It was hard to scare a man with threats of termination when his retirement check would be the same as his current take home pay, maybe a hair more.

"Sound serious Captain, lay it on me."

"Well you remember the kid that lost most of his ear when Cam took his gun away? His father has filed a complaint with the Chief about that and the Drug Checkpoint stops. I thought it would come from the councilman whose wife was stopped, but Councilman Gregory Santos decided to be the point guy on this one. He went straight to the Chief and the Chief went straight to me. I'm supposed to interview him personally, but I think I'll do that when you've completed your investigation."

Glen nodded, "Any insights you can give me on handling this one?"

"Well, you're gonna have to be creative to make this one go away. These council people just don't understand what we have to deal with every day. They lead a sheltered life, but then most people do. Here's his contact info." Johnson handed Glen a slip of paper with the phone number and address of the councilman. He added, "Bud, I don't have to tell you that the Chief has it out for your unit. He didn't come up through the ranks like the rest of us. He was a boy wonder that was hired to clean up things and he rides every political wave. I honestly fear this investigation more than any other I've seen."

Glen stood up and took the paper. "I'll be in touch."

Glen had one overriding mission, that consumed him lately. He needed to hand off the narc squad to competent management. He was planning on retirement and didn't want his baby to crash and burn. He'd taken great pride in building up the narc/gang squad and was proud of the cases they'd made over the years. He felt that he'd contributed great supervisors and important investigation to the department and even though some of the button-downed fussbudgets didn't like the free-wheeling narcs he knew what a valuable part of the force they were. This councilman thing was dangerous. Politics doesn't always follow law or logic. This could blow the whole unit to pieces and destroy the careers of some very fine officers. He trusted the Chief to do the right thing about as far as he could throw him.

∞

Cynthia Spencer didn't have even a small allotment of patience. She was so sick of the slowly grinding wheels of justice that she started a support group for the roofie rape victims. A couple dozen women gathered regularly to talk and help each other. Cynthia gave the contact, meeting times and location to Betty

Ward. Betty liked the idea even if the DA's office didn't. They believed the witnesses would contaminate each other's testimony, but Betty felt their mental health was more important. She figured they had the women's statements prior to the support group meeting and that was good enough to ensure some degree of non-contamination. And at this point she just didn't give a shit.

What no one counted on was that Cynthia and a few militant and very angry women decided to seek some justice on their own. Tamera Kohl was a website developer and she and Cynthia believed that everything about this case, including the suspect's personal information should be posted for public viewing. Power to the people via social media. Bradley Pope and Brian Defoe were about to experience all nine levels of Hell.

Defoe thought he heard a neighbor's dog barking last night, but that stupid mutt barks at every cat, bird and gust of wind, so he really didn't think much about it. When he opened his window at 9:00 am he saw the damage to his car. Along with four flat tires, someone had spray painted, "RAPIST" on his roof, fenders and back window with purple paint. When he went out to look at the car, he saw they had scratched, "PERVERT" into the front wind shield. It wasn't till he turned around to go back inside that he saw they had spray painted the same two words into the stucco siding of his home. They had taken a pair of pruning loppers to several small bushes in the front cutting them off at the ground in order to make the letters four feet high. They also cut his garden hose into pieces just for fun, as well as the valve stems on his car tires. Defoe thought of the George Carlin joke about how people locked away a few hundred dollars' worth of shit in their garage and leave a thirty-thousand-dollar car sitting outside. When he got inside, he heard his cell ringing. Bradley Pope received the same treatment. Their fun was just beginning.

∞

Lieutenant Glen thought it was time to check on a few things the squad was doing. He had confidence in the men and women assigned to him, but mentoring the next generation of leaders was a job that required fine tuning periodically. He told Cam that he'd come to their Tuesday morning supervisor meeting and that he needed an update on all their operations. Cam let his troops know, so they could be prepared. Glen wasn't patient with sloppy cops.

Cam opened the meeting once everyone trickled in. "I invited Terrence and Tommy for the first few minutes because they have their meth warrant signed and ready. After that we'll let them go and discuss Erin's roofie case and Bobby's 211 stake out." Everyone nodded.

Cam looked at Tommy and Terrence, then waited.

Terrence said, "Not sure why I'm here socializing with you narcs, but okay, I IDed this schmo Edwin Roberts by pretending it was just a traffic stop, and have continued tracking him from a distance. His dealing starts at about 10:00 am and goes till about 4:00 pm. Regular management hours. He takes Sundays off, if you can believe that."

Tommy added, "Todd and I chased down a few of his customers and have a sale to a minor charge we can slap on him when we're ready. Terrence and I will get our heads together and come up with a raid day and time. Right now, it's guess-work on when he'll be holding big."

Erin asked, "Weapons, priors, partners?"

Terrence answered, "He has several assaults on his rap sheet, probably customers that wouldn't pay up and one concealed/loaded possession charge from two years ago. He has a male roommate and it's hard to believe he's not involved somehow."

Cam nodded, "Any more questions? Okay guys, find a date and time and we'll do it." They got up and left.

Cam pointed at Erin, "You're up, we'll save the 211 for last because it's complicated."

Erin opened her large notebook and flipped through a few pages. "The DA's office is supposed to be coordinating everything, but they're having trouble keeping all these dogs on the porch. The victims have set up a support group headed by Cynthia Spenser and a member who's pretty tech savvy. Tamera Kohl has set up a web site outing everything about the case including all the personal information on our suspects. There have been several acts of vandalism against them and the threats have been pouring into their cells and email, all of which are posted on Kohl's rapist website. Their attorneys have been in touch with us asking for extra patrol.

Everyone at the table smiled, and Cam said, "When I mentioned that, at my patrol briefing, I got a round of snarky comments and laughs."

Erin added, "The problem that might rear its ugly head is Cynthia Spencer's dad. He's a retired cop and a bit of a hot head, I'm told. If he did something rash, he'd have a perfect alibi since they'd received so many death threats."

Everyone looked at Glen. "Ya, I know him. We worked detectives years ago. He is a hot head, or was. He's an old man now, but you never want to discount what a father will do when his daughter's been raped."

Cam asked everyone, "So, what do you guys see as our involvement in this case?"

Glen watched as a resident sociologist, wondering what this group of future leaders would come up with.

Erin said, "I don't think we have a lot of leverage to do much. The DA's office has the lead now. We're delegated to keeping the peace."

Bobby asked, "Does that include admonishing the victims and their families to be cool?"

Jesse laughed, "Like that is gonna influence anybody."

Glen said, "It might provide some cover if things get out of hand. At least we could answer from the witness stand that we warned any potential vigilantes to obey the law."

Cam looked at him, "If you want to talk with Spencer's father, Erin can contact the support group. I'll contact the media affairs officer and have him put something out."

Glen nodded, "Sounds good. What's next?"

Cam looked at Bobby, "Mr. Wright."

"Okay, the robbery stakeout operation is almost around the clock. When the grocery store is closed, we get a break, but they stay open late. The computer model and common sense tells us that it will go down over the three-day weekend coming up this month, but that's an educated guess. Ortiz's last 211 conviction was on a three-day weekend." Everyone smiled because they knew crooks often repeated their MO, because it was a way of trying to right a previous mistake and proving the validity of their original idea.

Bobby continued, "We've got Todd and Jesse qualified on the M4 rifle and SWAT loaned us two of their fortified vehicles to use in a takedown. They're plated to stop rounds and good for boxing vehicles in. If the crooks follow the dry run tactics we saw before, we'll need to have two sets of officers for each one of the suspect vehicles. I've made tentative assignments for that scenario. I've also assigned officers to clear civilians away from the scene to minimize stray rounds hitting someone or a potential hostage situation. Those plainclothes officers will be walking across the parking lot like shoppers when the crooks exit the store." Bobby paused for questions.

Erin asked, "Bobby how are you going to stop these guys from taking this mobile?"

"Our resident genius, Randy, bought a couple of tire boots that clamp onto a tire and stop the vehicle from going anywhere. We'll also use the armored SWAT vehicles to box them in on one side. I've assigned one shotgun to each crook vehicle with assorted ammo loads. They'll have bird shot, 00 buck and slugs, so they should be able to blow windows, tires, or punch holes in engines if need be."

Everyone was quiet for a moment waiting to see what else was asked.

Cam looked at Jesse. "Kahuna, why don't you explain what you've been up to."

Jesse nodded, "I've cranked out a rough draft search warrant on the gang house where Ortiz and his boys hang. We know all the facts in this case and the background information supplied by Bobby, Tommy, Cam and the crook's PO, so it's just a matter of filling in the final 211 information after it goes down. If it's pre-written, we should be able to hit the house quickly after the arrests and hopefully before the remaining dirt bags know we're coming. I'm guessing they'll leave lots of evidence of their preparation for the 211 and God knows what other offenses they've been involved in. I believe we could search it based on a parole search, but just to be safe, we'll have a warrant."

Lieutenant Glen looked at Cam. "And our parole officer liaison?"

Cam scratched the back of his head, "Ya, I agreed to contact him when this was over. He felt that his administrators would be less than pleased that he hadn't stopped this whole thing from going down. I'm trying not to cause him any problems."

Glen nodded, "Okay, I'm assuming that you'll use SWAT if there's time?"

Cam answered, "Right. Not likely, but that would be my first choice."

Glen stood and said, "Good luck," as he walked out.

CHAPTER 22

Erin had made her call to Cynthia Spencer and Tamera Kohl. She explained about their civil liability and asked them to be careful about invoking vigilante behavior. They both had received advice from legal counsel and politely told Erin goodbye. The media officer did his press release with the standard, "Let the justice system work" admonishment. That only left Lieutenant Glen to talk with Tony Spencer, the ex-cop whose daughter had been raped. Glen had several difficult phone calls to make this afternoon and he thought seriously about throwing his badge on the Captain's desk and riding his girlfriend and her sailboat to Saint Somewhere.

"Hello Tony, Bud Glen."

"Hi Bud. Thought I'd be hearing from you boys."

"Ya, sorry it took me so long. It's been a little nuts around here lately, as you can imagine. Look, I'm sorry about all this. It's a hard thing for a father to have to deal with and I wish I had a way to help, but sometimes life just sucks."

"I appreciate the call, Bud, and you guys did a good job of busting up this pack of assholes, but it would be great if they all did what the youngest one did and offed themselves."

"About that Tony, you're not thinking of doing something stupid are you?"

Quietly with no emotion Tony said, "No, Officer Glen, the thought never crossed my mind." The subsequent silence spoke loudly that Tony Spencer had been thinking exactly that, but as a well-educated cop he knew he should never admit it, especially if he had any plans to avenge his daughter's rape. The tactical way Tony Spencer answered Glen scared him. Glen knew that open threats or lengthy discussion was a sign of venting and probably meant nothing would happen. This behavior was troubling because it was exactly what Glen would do if he was going to kill the two rapists.

"Okay Tony, if there's anything you need, call me."

"Thanks for touching base, Bud, and tell that lady Sergeant of yours, thanks for helping my daughter."

Bud hung up and said to the dead phone, "Not good, not good at all."

∞

The next call Bud Glen had to make was easier emotionally, but still a huge pain in the ass.

"Good morning, Councilman Santos, this is Lieutenant Bud Glen from the police department. I've been assigned to investigate this complaint you've filed with the Chief's office."

Gregory Santos was cool and suspicious of getting the administrative pat on the head.

"Good morning, Lieutenant. I was told this investigation would be handled by Captain Johnson."

"Well Councilman, have you ever been in the military?"

"Yes, six years. Air Force."

Glen was surprised, six-year commitments often meant flight school. "Then you know all about how this works in a chain of command." He was going to say, "how shit rolls downhill," but thought Santos might think Glen believed his complaint was shit, even though his complaint was shit.

Santos didn't respond to Glen's comment and waited.

"Councilman, I assume you have a day job that occupies your schedule. How about we meet after work here at the department and we'll get some background information as a starter?"

"Okay, 6:00 would work for me."

"Great, come to the front entrance and ask for me. I'll tell them to expect you."

Glen then laid in a call to Cam. "Sergeant, we need to talk. You clear right now?"

Cam said, "would twenty minutes work?"

"Yes, my office," and Glen hung up.

When Cam arrived, Glen asked him about his planned activities for the evening.

"We're serving a search warrant on an apartment where Jesse's informant made some oxycodone buys and rotating a few narcs through our 211 gang stakeout.

"How about tomorrow?"

"Well, I think we're going to hit Tommy's meth dealer. The one he and Terrence have been working on that specializes in selling to the homeless folks."

Glen nodded and smiled, "That will work." Cam was a little confused.

Glen saw his look and said, "Let me explain. I've been assigned a personnel complaint naming you as the subject. Councilman Gregory Santos didn't care for it when you helped his son remove half of his ear. The straw that broke the councilman's back was the Drug Checkpoint arrest of his friend's wife."

Cam gritted his teeth, "Crap."

Glen agreed, "Right, and lots of it. This is one of those moments in life where doing the same thing in the same way and expecting different results is extra stupid. We can't make this guy go away with a standard law enforcement explanation. We need to do a bold adjustment. The councilman needs to see the world the way we do, and the only way that's going to happen is if he lives in our world for a while. So, here's what you're going to do. After he and I talk tonight in my office I'll hit you on the air and we'll 11-98. I'll pass him off to you and you show him what we do. Take him with you everywhere and use him like a grunt narc, searching, logging crook plates, on code 5's, the whole bit. Don't worry about him getting hurt and don't pull any punches. I think he's a former Air Force pilot based on a couple of clues. That would mean he's not a pussy. I'll tell him he can interview you personally about your tactics at his son's arrest and the check point stops. Lay it out straight to him."

Cam, with a questioning look on his face said, "You sure this is a good idea?"

"No, but Captain Johnson believes this is a huge bomb we're hatching under our asses and this just might work if the guy's got any character at all."

"Okay, Lieutenant, how's that saying go? No guts, no glory."

Cam had always thought a cop should have a backup career. You never knew in police work when the bottom was going to fall out. He knew a lot of good cops that had to start another job for no reason they could control. Sometimes it was an injury, sometimes an internal investigation. They lived in a world where justice wasn't always just. Cam's way of guarding against poverty was to get his teaching credential. He liked kids and even though a teacher's salary wasn't great, it would allow him to survive. A backup career was especially critical now that he had a family.

CHAPTER 23

Two of the women from Cynthia Spencer's support group who were also victims of Defoe and Bradley went for a walk at 10:00 am one morning. They had been following the court calendar carefully and saw that the defendants had a 'motion to suppress' hearing, that day, which would mean they weren't going to be home. They covered their faces with a stocking cap and put on big sunglasses just in case someone had video monitors working. As they walked by Brian Defoe's home they stepped around the side of his house and walked toward the rear. They squatted down to their knees and removed a battery-operated drill with an exceptionally long shank from a backpack. They drilled a large hole in the side of his house penetrating all the way through the exterior wall and insulation into his living room. They were going to use his hose to water the house but they'd cut it up last time they were here, so they borrowed the neighbor's hose. They screwed it on the facet that was a few feet away, poked it through the hole they drilled and opened the valve wide open. Then they went to Bradley Pope's house and did the same thing.

∞

Jesse's oxycodone search warrant was developed after he had an informant buy from the crook on two different occasions. He recruited the informant because a fishing buddy of his working patrol caught the guy holding a couple of oxycodone pills in a baggy. The cop knew that if the guy had a prescription, he wouldn't be carrying them that way and that dealers often sold them in baggies. The crook admitted to scoring them in town, but wouldn't tell the cop where. That's where Jesse came in. He could offer the guy a break on the charges if he cooperated. Jesse gave him marked money, searched him to make sure he was drug free and sent him into the house to buy the dope. Both times he returned to Jesse with a baggy of five pills that cost fifty bucks. Jesse gathered the crew and would hit the house at about 7:00 pm. He figured after analyzing the informant's information that it would be a likely time to catch the crook holding. Timing was critical with search warrants. You had to catch them with dope because you weren't charging the sales, only the possession. More than a few cases fell apart because the cops timing was off and the crook was out of dope.

∞

Lieutenant Glen escorted Gregory Sanchez back to his office and asked him to have a seat. Sanchez was not openly hostile, but it was obvious to Glen that he was prepared to be jerked around. Glen didn't fault his attitude; that's generally what government did to people when they were a problem.

"Councilman Sanchez, I was told by Captain Johnson to cooperate fully with you on this investigation and that's exactly what I intend to do. The preliminary report you filed states you're concerned about the use of force and adherence to professional standards. I think a good way to proceed is for you to have access to the officers involved directly. That way you can ask them any questions you'd like without their explanations being filtered by another party. Since you are a councilman and have asked to have an investigation as a councilman, you have a duty to the city to not place it in legal jeopardy, therefore I have no problem sharing all the case information with you. I've got two release forms for you to get signed by your son and your councilman friend's wife. Once those are signed, I can give you full copies of the arrest reports, so you can have more detailed information on which to base your questions of the officers involved. Does sound acceptable to you?"

Gregory Sanchez was blown away. He didn't expect this level of cooperation and access. "Yes Lieutenant, that will be fine. I, uh, I'm a bit surprised."

Glen smiled, "Well there is a catch." Sanchez face hardened. "My people are extremely busy right now and we have several critical cases that can't wait. Search warrants can expire, robberies are about to go down and crooks are selling poison to the citizens, some of them children, so I'll need you to talk with the officers in the field."

Glen decided that he'd set Sanchez up with his next statement. "I noted you were a pilot in the Air Force, so it's a given that you're not a coat-and-tie pussy like a lot of politicians. My men will get you the equipment you need and I think you'll get better information from them if they actually get to know you. Will that work?"

Sanchez was in a mild state of shock. "Yes, that's fine."

Glen stood up, "Here's a liability waiver for you to sign in case you get shot. Sign it and give it to the Sergeant. Follow me and I'll introduce you."

Glen got up and walked past the councilman on his way to the narc squad room. Sanchez followed with his fistful of paperwork wondering what he'd just gotten himself into.

Glen and Sanchez walked into the squad room just after Cam had started the search warrant briefing. Jesse was going over a sketch of the house they were going to hit using a pen on a white board.

Glen walked up to Cam and said, "This is Gregory Sanchez. He's to have full access and answer all his questions." Cam nodded his head and Glen walked out.

Cam shook Sanchez's hand and said, "Have a seat while we do this briefing and then we'll get you all set up." Sanchez wasn't quite sure what "all set up" meant.

Jesse was explaining to the squad where all the doors were located and making assignments to cover them. He went through the dope they were looking for and made a point of locating the one toilet in this house because that's where they'd try to flush the dope if they could.

He started to give what information he had about the occupants and it made everyone slightly nervous. "The crook is afraid of a rip-off because oxycodone users are desperate types, so he's likely to have guns nearby. My informant saw one on top of the refrigerator. He also has two kids, a big angry wife and other assorted knot heads hanging around the house, so we've got to be quick, careful and move fast through the whole place to secure it."

Randy said, "What, no magic plan to neutralize their superpowers? Did you not think to call me?"

Jesse fired back, "I do have a great idea about how you could be useful. We could have Todd throw you through the back window like a javelin and you could shoot all the crooks as you fly past them."

Everyone laughed as Todd made a javelin throwing motion.

Cam spoke up, "Focus gentlemen."

Jesse, smiling, said, "My plan to seize this place a little faster than usual is to have our radio open on the tactical net so a rear entry team can hit the back door at the same time we hit the front. That means everybody's got to stay frisky and watch for good guys. We'll all have raid vests, but remember to watch for a crossfire situation."

Tommy asked, "Who's point on the back door?"

"Todd and you, Tommy."

Tommy looked at Todd and did a couple of head bobs. Todd smiled and did another javelin motion.

Sanchez watched, listened and thought. He hadn't heard this kind of banter since his flight briefing days in the Air Force. He smiled.

∞

Jesse was assigning vehicles and officers to arrive at their assigned locations, so Cam Told Sanchez to follow him.

Cam handed Sanchez a pen and said, "Sign that waiver so we can get you shot without paying and I'll get you a vest. Randy, do you still have your old body armor in your locker?" Randy had been given a new, very expensive T-shirt vest by his parents for his birthday.

"Ya, it might not smell like violets in spring time, but it will still work."

"Good, I need to borrow it for our guest here."

"Sure, I'll go grab it. I've got to get some gear anyway."

Cam said, "Take him with you to the locker room and get him fixed up. And Randy, don't give him all your ideas about city improvements on his first visit."

Randy frowned and turned both hands out, "What, me?"

When all the squad units arrived at the crook's house, they were already on the secure tactical radio net. Cam had Sanchez with him and he was looking a little overwhelmed.

"Okay Jesse, this is your baby, tell us when."

Jesse, keyed his mic. "Todd and Tommy, get in position, then let me know. Cam, you and Al are behind me."

Everyone exited their cars and guns were removed and held in a low ready position, pointed down and out at a 45-degree angle. Sanchez had an "Oh Shit!" moment. Things were getting serious. Everyone slid in beside the doors of the house remembering to not stand in front of the door. That's were bullets were aimed. Cam put a hand across Sanchez's chest pushing him behind a door casing for cover.

Tommy hit the radio, "We're in place."

Jesse said, "10-4."

He knocked on the door and the whole house became quiet except for a TV in the background.

"Who's there?"

Jesse figured any name he gave would probably be wrong, so he just knocked again. The voice on the other side of the door was now standing just behind the door.

"Who is it?"

Jesse looked at Cam and shrugged, "I'm Jesse Hale from the police department and I have a search warrant for your house."

All hell broke loose. People started running and screaming as Jesse raised one extremely large foot and hit the door right beside the knob and lock. The wooden door jamb split, but the door was still closed. Cam caught Jesse with his left hand as he started to fall backwards and pushed him upright again. Jesse hit it one more time and it flew open. The dealer was trying to hold the door shut with his hands, but this 140 lb. guy was no match for a 240 lb. narc. The door hit him square in the face, knocking him on his butt. Jesse stepped in and picked the guy up by his shirt and pants, flipping him on his belly for cuffing. The crook tried to get up, but Jesse dropped onto his back with a knee causing the crook to lose his wind, so cuffing was easy.

Meanwhile out back Todd had blown his door to pieces with one good kick from his tactical boot and he and Tommy were proceeding through the house yelling, "Police Officer-Search Warrant."

Cam, with Sanchez right behind, went over the top of Jesse as he was cuffing the dealer in an attempt to get to any other occupants that might be flushing dope or going for guns.

Al joined Tommy and Todd doing the same thing from the rear door. Tommy and Todd headed down a hall way where two bedrooms were located and split up to each take one while Al went the other direction toward the kitchen.

As Cam and Sanchez were about to enter the kitchen through a closed swinging door, they heard Al yell, "Touch that gun and you're dead! On your knees, hands behind your head! Now!"

Cam skidded to a halt at the side of the door, "Al, clear to enter?"

"Clear."

As Cam and Sanchez opened the kitchen door, they saw Al with his gun pointed at a 20 something male who was kneeling in front of the refrigerator. A 41-magnum revolver was right above his head.

Al said, "Cam, cuff him." Cam pinched the crook's fingers together with his left hand and applied the cuffs with his right. Al holstered his weapon and grabbed the cuffed prisoner to take him out to the living room where all the arrested occupants were searched and seated on the floor. As he passed Cam and Sanchez he said, "He was reaching for the gun when I came in behind him, but don't sweat the possibilities, I'm almost sure your vest would stop a magnum like that. I think. Maybe. It's possible."

Cam replied with a nod and a frown. Sanchez said, "Funny guy."

Cam said, "Ya, amazing how many cops think they're comedians."

Cam walked over to the sliding glass door that Erin was assigned to watch and flipped the latch, allowing her to slide it open.

She looked round, "What'd I miss?"

Jesse shrugged, "Just another group of satisfied customers. You want to start organizing a search?"

"Sure, you read the Miranda and the warrant and I'll make some room assignments."

After about a half hours' worth of searching they found the drug stash. The kitchen had fluorescent lights with a plastic diffuser covering them. The baggies of dope were hidden behind the lip.

Cam asked Jesse, "How much, Kahuna?"

Fifty bags of five each. Five must be the going sale amount. Get this, Al found dozens of empty baggy containers in the trash along with a dated grocery store receipt for their purchase. We should be able to estimate a sales amount based on the number of baggies times five pills."

Cam laughed. "Master criminal. Don't forget to notify IRS and Franchise Tax. I'm guessing he didn't pay taxes on his business income."

Just as Jesse was getting ready to bag up some evidence there was a knock on the broken door they'd pushed back in place. Everyone was quiet while Jesse opened it a few inches. A white male about 35 looked at Jesse and saw the dealer setting on a couch with his hands not visible, cuffed behind his back.

He said, "Hey dude, you got any oxy left, I need to score a few?"

The dealer couldn't believe this idiot and said, looking at Jesse, "He's got them."

Jesse said, "How many you want?" The guy handed Jesse a twenty-dollar bill. Jesse handed the guy two pills he pulled out of a baggy.

The guy said, "Cool man," and started to leave. That's when Jesse badged him, seized the two pills and cuffed him.

Everyone broke out laughing except the dealer, who said "Idiot."

Al commented, "So much for the, 'I'm not a dealer' defense."

Cam found Erin and told her, "I'm going to split and see how Bobby and Randy are doing on the 211 stakeout. You got this?"

"Ya, Jesse and I'll handle it. Those guys on the code 5 probably could use a break."

Cam, with his new shadow in tow, crawled into his car. "I need to give these guys a break so they can get something to eat and use the restroom. They usually take some food with them and a bottle to pee in, but they always prefer to live like civilized humans, so they'll appreciate the relief. It will give you and I a chance to talk. As soon as you get those individual waivers signed by your son and the councilman's wife I can talk about those specific cases, but we can talk about tactics, department procedures and everything else."

Sanchez was starting to like these guys. He hadn't counted on that.

CHAPTER 24

Cynthia Spencer wasn't just waiting for justice from the courts. She was a proactive kind of person. The Superior Court Judge who set bail for Bradley Pope and Brian Defoe was now under scrutiny from ladies who volunteered at the women's crisis shelter. There was a general belief amongst activist women that the courts didn't take sexual assault seriously enough and so it was Cynthia's goal to hold everyone, --courts, DA's office and law enforcement--accountable for their behavior.

She also planned to use Tamera Kohl's computer skills to keep the outrage alive. Tamera came across as an air-head nerd, but her attention to detail on the website showed a disciplined mind. She knew that the public had a short attention span, so Tamera opened a chat room about rape and sexual assault. There was a never-ending stream of victims ready to share their stories. The blog that was attached gave daily updates on the case and reports on how all the government agencies were responding. Pictures of and full backgrounds on the suspects were updated regularly. After Brian Defoe was punched in the nose at a gas station by a large angry woman, his attorney threatened to sue the women involved in the website. They posted that threat also and all the information about his attorney and his legal practice.

Lieutenant Glen told Captain Johnson, "This shit is getting ugly, personal, and very interesting."

The Captain offered, "These women might represent a bigger deterrent than prison."

∞

Cam and Sanchez pulled in beside Bobby's car. "You boys need food and bladder relief?"

Randy answered, "Hell yes, on both."

Bobby said, "Nothing much going down here. Two of the guys we saw with Ortiz on the dry run robbery just drove in. We could use another car here in case these guys split up."

Cam said, "Ya, I'll hit Erin on the air and have her send a couple of guys. She's almost done on the oxycodone warrant."

Randy asked, "How'd you do?"

"Fifty bags of five each. All kinds of sales evidence."

Randy smacked the steering wheel, "Excellent." Just as he was getting ready to tell Cam they'd be right back the front door of the gang house opened. "Heads up guys, we got activity."

Ortiz and two other gang members got into the car that just arrived and backed out of the driveway.

Cam said, "Bobby, guess we'll take them and you call Erin for some assistance."

"Okay, you sure you don't need Randy. I can spare him, you know?"

Randy said, "Hey, I heard that. Hand me that empty Gatorade bottle would ya. The big one."

Cam smiled as he drove away.

As Cam followed Ortiz and his buddies down the street, he made sure to stay as far back as he could without losing sight of them. He explained to Sanchez what he was doing and why, including his tactic of surveilling the gang members because of the robbery information they'd gathered. He didn't hold much back from the councilman. He wanted him to know how dangerous these guys were and what a threat they represented to the public.

"Homicide believes this parolee Ortiz burned up a previous gang leader for stealing from the gang, but they couldn't prove it and they sure can't get a witness because everyone saw what happens to guys who fuck with Ortiz. The autopsy said he was alive when someone poured gas on him and lit the match."

Sanchez said nothing, but thought, "So we're playing hide and seek with him, swell."

"Cam, I don't like being out here doing all this stuff with you......"

Cam was just about to think this guy might be a coward, when he finished the sentence.

".... without a gun. How do we fix that?"

Cam thought for a minute, "Well, the Lieutenant didn't discuss that with me and I'm not sure you'd be authorized or covered for us to allow that."

Sanchez was quiet as he watched Cam reached down and pull up his left pant leg. He removed his backup gun a, Ruger LCR .357 and slid it into the deep pocket of the center console where Sanchez could reach it.

"I'll talk with Glen about that problem tomorrow."

The three gang members pulled up in front of a Pawn shop near the freeway on-ramp and went inside.

"Cam was perplexed, "What the fuck is this?" Cam hit Erin on the air, "N8, N6."

"Go ahead."

"I'm at a pawn shop near Story Road and Lucretia watching Ortiz and two of his boys. Can you break a couple of squad members loose to assist?"

"Affirmative, Al and Todd are en route to relieve Bobby. I can send them your way."

Cam answered, "No, keep them going. I'll have Bobby 11-98 here."

Erin, Bobby and Al all responded that they copied the radio traffic. Al and Todd relieved Bobby and Randy. When Bobby arrived, he and Randy jumped in Cam's car.

Randy said, "Sup dudes?"

Cam shook his head, "Ortiz and two other gang members just went into that pawn shop and I'm trying to figure out why."

Randy gave a one-word answer: "Guns."

Bobby added, "That's probably a good guess. They can't pull off a major 211 without serious weapons. They have to look scary and be capable of winning a firefight. And they can't come back registered to anybody."

Cam looked at Bobby, "Have you guys got any field glasses or infrared vision opticals?"

Bobby looked at Randy, "Is a duck's butt water-tight? Of course." Randy opened a small backpack he always carried and pulled out a pair of night vision field glasses.

Cam told Randy, "Okay, Inspector Gadget, I need to know who those other guys are. Your gang folder Bobby put together should have almost everyone's photo in it. You two take your car and position it closer by that dumpster. We'll stay here and see what happens."

Bobby and Randy drove across the street to get Randy a better vantage point and hid their car. Randy got out and positioned himself behind a bush with his field glasses. Randy, being Randy, found a box in the dumpster to sit on and covered his head and upper body with a dark blanket he found in the undercover car. Bobby was amazed. Not only was Randy warm, but he was almost invisible.

Forty-five minutes later the three thugs exited the store without carrying anything. They got into their car and pulled away.

Cam hit Bobby on the radio, "We'll take the car. You two watch the store and see if you can get an eyeball on the clerk and any vehicle he's driving."

"10-4."

Bobby got out of the car and met Randy on his way back. "Go back and see if you can ID the clerk. Plate numbers on his ride and his face in your memory bank." Randy nodded and returned to his box.

Ten minutes later the clerk shut off the lights and locked the front door. As he walked to his car, Randy got a clear shot of his face. He was Caucasian, 30's, 160 lbs. and about five feet and a couple of inches tall. Randy had a trick for remembering what people looked like. He'd try to match them with a movie star.

He was a big TV and movie fan and usually found a close lookalike. After the guy drove away Randy wrote down his plate number. They would get the registration info and find a driver's license photo to confirm his identity.

Cam decided that Ortiz was going to bed for the night and Bobby followed the clerk for twenty minutes and put him to bed. Erin had wrapped up the search warrant and folded the gang house surveillance till the next morning. She figured as long as the grocery store was closed, they couldn't rob it. She really hoped that they didn't have their eye on another place.

As everyone trickled into the squad room Cam gave one final order to his troops: "Sleep."

He looked at Sanchez and said, "We didn't get a lot of time to talk, but we'll do this again. Most of the time we have a little slack, it's just that right now everything's hitting us at once. Call my cell anytime to make sure I'm not on days off or have court and we'll do this again."

Sanchez said, "Okay, thanks." As he walked away, he wasn't sure what to make of his experience tonight. It wasn't what he expected and it left him a little confused.

CHAPTER 25

Meeting Betty Ward at the courthouse was an accident. Erin was there to testify on an old drug case, but just as she was getting ready to go on the stand the Deputy DA told her to go home. The defendant's attorney decided to plead him guilty and took the deal that was offered a week ago.

Betty was getting some court papers assigning her to interview a victim of domestic violence.

Betty walked out of the court clerk's office right in front of Erin.

"Hi, Betty."

"Erin, what brings you to court. Fighting crime?"

"Ya, but he plead guilty, so I prepped for nothing."

"Good, you'll have time for coffee with me then."

"Sure, I promise not to use you for therapy."

Betty laughed, "Okay, how about I use you?"

Erin wondered what that was about. Betty was famous for entering important conversations from the back door. As they sat down, they chatted about gossip and a mutual friend of theirs who was running for a local political office. Erin waited. She knew Betty was grazing around the subject she wanted to talk about and she was going to let Betty get to it her way.

"So, Erin how are you doing with this roofie rape case?"

"Well, we've done about all we can at the PD. Now it's just a matter of the slow grinding wheels of justice. Not that there's not a lot of side shows going on."

"That's what I wanted to talk with you about." Erin folded her hands in her lap and smiled politely at Betty, waiting. "You know I've kind of developed a counselor type relationship with these women?"

"Yes, I knew that."

"We meet almost weekly so they can talk and support one another and let off a little steam. The justice process, as we both know, is ponderously frustrating." Erin nodded her agreement. "I have a bit of a conflict I need to deal with and I was hoping you might help."

Erin sipped her coffee and said, "I'll try."

"I know you will, dear. I'm required professionally to keep client information confidential, but I'm required legally to inform law enforcement if I feel a serious crime is going to be committed. Sometimes it's a narrow balancing act that leaves me less than sure of the correct route to travel." Betty paused as if she were thinking this over. Erin waited patiently. "One of the ladies in my group commented to me privately that she wouldn't have to wait for justice until the trial. She went on at great length about how the system was victimizing her all over again and that things were already in motion to exact justice. I won't reveal her identity, but I have sufficient knowledge of her circumstances to believe this is not an idle threat. I must confess, I have mixed feelings about this. I've seen so many women treated like crap on the witness stand that I understand her attitude completely, but professionally I just can't ignore this."

"Anything else you can tell me, Betty?"

"No, not really."

Erin paused a moment, "Well, Betty, you haven't given me enough information to justify any law enforcement action. And while you might feel absolved, I suspect this conversation changes nothing. All it does is give me an, 'Oh that's what Betty was talking about,' moment sometime in the future."

Betty looked down at her hands and said, "You really are a hard ass, aren't you?"

Erin laughed, "So I'm told."

Betty stood up and said, "I have to go, dear. Thanks, I guess."

∞

Cam called a squad meeting to discuss the progress on the investigations they had running. Lieutenant Glen couldn't make it, so he told Cam to write up a briefing paper on the items discussed.

"Bobby, give us a heads up on the pawn shop clerk."

"Adam Alquist, he has two DUI's and lots of petty charges over the last ten years, malicious mischief, theft, and marijuana. He's 5' 4" 155 lbs., 32 years of age. Looks like he's just the hired help, but the owner is seldom in the shop according to the landlord I talked with, so Alquist basically manages the place. I had Randy stroll through the store like a customer and he says there's guns enough to arm a small revolution. If I had to guess, this is where Ortiz will get his armament. I've got Randy checking right now with ATF, to see if they've got anything on this operation."

Cam nodded, "And the 211?"

Bobby continued, "Not much new. We keep rotating surveillance on the gang house when the Safeway is open, but all indications are that the three-day weekend is when it's happening. I think we're prepared. We've got vehicles, equipment and everybody trained and assigned, so it's stand-by till the event."

Cam looked at Erin and Jesse, "You two have been keeping track of the meth dealer case Tommy's handling, right?"

Jesse gestured to Erin, "Ya, Terrence and Tommy say they're ready and that it could go down tonight or tomorrow if our sources say he's holding. Looks like a standard warrant, but I think we're going to need a few bodies because the area to be searched is extensive."

Cam asked, "Any tactical issues?"

Erin pointed at Jesse, "Edwin Roberts gives every impression of being a runner. He's done it on prior police contacts. We don't know anything about his roommate because he's not on the utilities and doesn't own a car that we know of. Any more investigation is liable to burn us, so we backed off."

Cam said, "Okay, let me know when we're a go."

"I'm going to have Sanchez with me again tonight."

Bobby asked, "How's that going?"

Cam shrugged, "Hard to tell, he's really quiet most the time and hasn't asked a lot of questions. I think he might be a little overwhelmed. What's normal to us is pretty crazy to the uninitiated."

Everyone nodded their agreement. "Anything else, guys?"

Erin said, "Ya, you should probably let the Lieutenant know that I had a talk with Betty Ward and she believes someone is planning to do something permanent to our rapists sometime in the future."

Jesse sarcastically said, "Really have it nailed down, do you?"

Erin shrugged, "Well, she wasn't very forthcoming because she was concerned about professional ethics and client confidentiality."

Cam said, "Okay, will do." As he got up, he said, "Let's go make the streets safe for humanity."

CHAPTER 26

Sanchez met Cam in the squad room and was wearing Randy's old body armor under his flannel shirt. Cam shook his hand and signaled for him to have a seat. Tommy was getting ready for a briefing on the meth dealer search warrant they were going to serve tonight. Terrence was handing out a diagram of the house and property with pictures of Edwin Roberts.

Erin spoke up so everyone chattering could hear, "Listen up gentleman, Tommy's ready to start." Everyone quieted down and Tommy diagramed the house and grounds. He was the lead investigator on the warrant, so he would do the Knock and Notice at the front door. Tradition had it that the point man got to pick his entry partner. You always want to pick a tactically sound officer because going through the front door is the dangerous part of the warrant service. Tommy picked Cam and Terrence. Todd and Randy were assigned the rear door and Erin, Jesse and Al would be in position at a side entrance. Nothing was known about weapons.

Tommy told the squad, "I'm not comfortable with how little we know about the crook and this house, but there really isn't any way to find out more without burning ourselves. This guy's super paranoid, so we have to get at him without much investigation. He should be home tonight and we still have a few hours of daylight. Our source tells us he should be holding a week's supply of meth."

Erin asked, "Okay, any questions?"

No one said anything, so Randy jumped up and said, "To the Batmobile."

Everyone laughed and Erin shook her head. "He never runs out."

It was about a twenty-minute drive to get to the crook's house and Cam took his car with councilman Sanchez. "So, councilman, did you get those folks, your son and the other councilman's wife to sign those waivers?"

"Cam, please call me Greg. And no, there was a problem there." Cam had an idea what the problem was, but let it go.

"Well, Greg, I have a legal problem discussing arrests without a waiver even with your son because he's an adult and has privacy rights. I could get sued for talking about their personal cases."

"I know. It's not your problem, it's mine. I'll keep any questions I have generic."

Cam nodded.

"Cam, did you have a chance to talk with Lieutenant Glen about me being armed?"

"Yes, and he referred me to Captain Jenkins who said we could issue you a concealed permit after you complete the application process." Sanchez frowned. "Ya, I know, so I think we'll handle it like we've been handling it." Cam placed a revolver in a holster in the center console pocket. Sanchez nodded, leaving it there.

All the individual units arrived at the end of Edwin Roberts's street, and they jumped into three cars for the final approach. Tommy, Cam and Terrence went first, followed by Todd and Randy. Jesse, Erin and Al went in the third car. As they pulled up in front of the dealer's house, they saw him and his roommate running out the front door and back toward the rear alley.

Cam hit the radio, "Todd, go right. Erin, take the house. We'll go left." The squad wasn't sure how the crooks knew they were coming, but they did. Now the question was which way they went down the alley. Once they were behind the house the narcs couldn't tell. As the three squad cars split in three directions all the narcs jumped out and began to run.

Tommy ran faster than Cam and Terrence which is why he just got a sliver of Roberts's profile as he headed back toward the street they'd driven in on. As Tommy rounded the corner of the end house, he saw the crook cross the street and drop into a truck yard. The entire block across the street from Edwin Roberts's house was a commercial truck yard for a refrigerated transport truck line. They had a huge loading dock that overlooked a warehouse storage area below. Tommy told Cam and Terrence that he didn't see anyone else with Roberts, so he suspected the two roommates split up and the other guy went right. Cam got on the radio and told Todd to keep going and that he was going to search the truck yard for whoever he could find. Todd acknowledged while he was running down the alley.

Todd couldn't see any way for the other crook to make it between houses, so he ran all the way to the end and made a right to search the truck dock from the opposite end.

Meanwhile Erin radioed Cam that the house was secure and they'd started searching. Erin put Jesse on watch in case Roberts or his buddy returned.

Cam decided that Roberts probably won't want to get caught on the high overlook where all the truck trailers had been backed in. The truck yard attempted to make theft from the trailers difficult by backing the rear of them over a ten-foot-high wall that was above the ramp area leading into the warehouse. There weren't a lot of places to hide on the high side unless you crawled up under a trailer. As Cam, Terrence, Tommy and Sanchez slowed down and picked their way through boxes, piles of pallets and forklifts, they thought about the dangers of an ambush. This was a long and wide loading area with hundreds of hiding places.

Cam grabbed Sanchez by the upper arm and said, "You need to stay right behind me. Do not get ahead of me. Understand?"

Sanchez nodded.

Terrence fanned out to the right and Cam stayed left. Tommy took the middle. They went slowly, trying to move from cover to cover. When they couldn't find something that would stop bullets, they opted for something that would hide them. Sanchez thought how this was like a fighter formation when they had an enemy sighting on radar.

Todd and Randy decided that based on Cam's last radio transmission they would go in on the high side. The crook was blocked on the low side by the warehouse and they didn't want to get in a crossfire situation if people started shooting. Besides, if the other crook came this way he was probably under a truck unless he jumped down ten feet to the warehouse ramp. Randy went on the back side where the trailers overhung the wall. Todd went on the opposite end. They both went slowly, so nobody could get between them. The noise on the truck dock was loud. All the refrigeration units were running which would hide the sound of their movements but also stop communications.

Todd looked over at Randy and saw him signal with his right hand like a traffic cop to stop. Todd stopped and watched as Randy dropped to his back under a trailer, which gave him a view under about three or four trailers. He jumped up and signaled Todd to move forward. Both groups of narcs continued their search, slowly and methodically. Randy would drop down every so often on his back and look under the row of trailers. After about twelve trailers Randy dropped again and Todd noticed he didn't move for an extra long time. Todd watched and waited. He always gave Randy a hard time about all his crazy ideas, but he actually respected how smart he was and how he took all the teasing with a sense of humor. Randy stood up and pointed with his left hand at the trailer he was facing and put up one finger. Then he put up four fingers and pointed directly up with his left. Todd put up four fingers in response and Randy nodded. They moved slowly and quietly past the other trailers and when they got to number four Todd signaled to Randy that he'd go around it to the other side.

When Randy saw Todd's legs across from his he dropped to the ground, pointed his gun at the crook and yelled, "Freeze, Police!" The crook was trying to decide whether to comply or run when Todd latched onto his leg with what the crook though was a vise. He'd holstered his gun with his right hand and grabbed the same ankle for a two-handed grip. Todd did one handed curls with 80 lbs., so with a little adrenaline in his veins it was no surprise that the crook came flying loose when Todd gave a mighty jerk. The crook's head smacked into a steel beam that was part of the trailer frame, stunning him slightly. Todd pulled the guy out from under the trailer on his side and Randy crawled under rather than running around the front. The two narcs stood the crook up and Randy saw a large Ziplock baggie protruding from the front of the crook's pants. Randy pulled it out and saw that it was a one-pound baggie with several dozen smaller baggies of meth. Apparently, the crooks didn't want it found in the house and thought they'd be able to ditch the cops. As Todd was searching the guy for weapons before he cuffed him, Randy saw something down below on the lower loading dock. It was Cam, Sanchez, Tommy and Terrence who were slowly making their way along the dock, guns out moving from cover to cover. As Randy looked left to where they were headed, he could see below him and about 20 feet out Edwin Roberts crouched down and hidden amongst a pile of empty cardboard boxes. He had a gun out and was pointing it at the approaching officers. Randy waived his arms and yelled, "Cam, Gun!"

That got Todd's attention and he hurried to the edge of the wall with his uncuffed prisoner in tow.

Randy repeated it as loud as he could yell and jumped up and down waving his arms yelling, "Cam, Gun!" But the roar of the refrigeration units blocked out everything. Neither Roberts nor the narcs could hear him. Randy looked around for something to throw at Cam to get his attention, but couldn't find anything. The place was sterile. He had just decided that he'd draw his weapon and shoot the boxes around Roberts. Cam and Terrence would surely hear gunfire and if nothing else it would scare the crook. He was giving serious thought to just shooting Roberts. It would be a legal shooting based on the facts. He'd drawn his gun thinking two rounds for the boxes and if he doesn't drop the gun, then two into Roberts.

Just then, he saw human being, flying through the air, headed towards Roberts. Todd had grabbed his prisoner by the back of his belt with his right hand and the guy's jacket with his left and did a clean and jerk body lift with him. Then he'd stepped over to the edge of the dock with him overhead, and threw him with all his might at Edwin Roberts. The flying guy with his arms flailing almost seemed to float for a few seconds before landing smack on top of Roberts, breaking Roberts's collar bone and knocking him unconscious.

Cam, Terrence, Tommy and Sanchez weren't quite sure what just happened. When they looked up, they saw Randy and Todd waiving at them. After they cuffed both prisoners, they had an ambulance transport them for medical treatment. The prisoner Todd threw was miraculously uninjured except where he hit his head being pulled from under the truck. The piles of cardboard boxes and Roberts had largely absorbed the fall. The guy couldn't remember much because he was wasted on meth and had been drinking heavily to stop his heart from racing, which is standard self-medication for cranksters. The bang on the head from being pulled from under the trailer didn't help either.

Todd kept telling him, "You've got to be a crazy mother fucker to jump off a wall like that." By the time he'd told the guy that a dozen times, he believed it. Roberts didn't know what hit him. One minute he was waiting in ambush for some cops, the next he was out cold.

Cam said, "I can't wait to read this report. It'll be right up there with the time you scalped that kid and taped his pony-tail to your locker."

Todd said, "It's not my fault, you know. All that Javelin talk got stuck in my head."

Terrence was in hysterics, "I swear, you people are the most insane pack of psycos the department ever created. I keep asking myself why I work with you nuts. Well, this is why. You're more fun than a pack of monkeys in a bounce house." He was laughing so hard he had trouble getting up from the box he was sitting on.

Sanchez couldn't help himself. He busted up laughing too.

When they had all the crooks transported to the hospital with Todd and Al escorting them, the remaining narcs went to Roberts's house. Jesse and Erin had gathered up a ton of evidence and a lot of intelligence on Roberts's dope connection. They also found two more one-pound Ziplock bags with individual baggies inside.

Jesse called Cam, "Commander Cameron, take a look at this." He was looking at a closed-circuit TV picture on Robert's computer which showed four views of the outside, two out the front and two of the alley, behind the house. "That's how he knew we were coming."

Cam shook his head, "Technology is making life complicated Jesse."

Jesse smiled, "No shit."

∞

The next day Councilman Gregory Sanchez asked Lieutenant Glen if he had a moment and of course Glen said he did. They met in Glen's office right after 5:00 pm.

"Lieutenant, I just wanted to tell you that I've completed my fact-finding mission."

Glen said, "Okay."

"You do know, Lieutenant, that your people are insane."

"Yes, I've thought the same thing myself on a number of occasions, but you can't help but like and respect them, can you?"

"No, you can't. You set me up. Everything from asking for waivers from my son and the lady lawyer, to riding with them on these crazy raids."

"Ya, I guess I did, but you wouldn't have believed me if I told you the complainants wouldn't want you to read about their conduct. You have to see evidence like that on your own. You can't describe our job to an outsider. They have to experience it. I knew when I met you and heard your background that you'd understand quickly."

"I'll talk with your Chief tomorrow and make this thing go away. I only have one regret about the whole adventure."

What's that councilman?"

"That my son couldn't have ended up like one of them."

Glen didn't know what to say, so he said nothing.

Sanchez saw Cam on his way out of the police department, "Cam, thanks for the tour. It was enlightening."

Cam said, "Sure, anytime. You ought to think about becoming a reserve. The guys like you."

Sanchez smiled and waved as he walked away.

Cam stepped into Glen's office to update him on all the latest events, "So, where we at with Sanchez's complaint?"

"He says you're insane. I agreed. Now give me an update."

CHAPTER 27

Cam and the other supervisors were glad to have some of these cases at an end point. There wasn't much to do on the rape case and Tommy's meth warrant was a wrap except for court. Now they could concentrate on Ortiz and the 211 operation. He asked Erin and the SWAT commander Lieutenant Tomasovic to look over the tactical plans Bobby created just to see if they missed anything. He recognized that this was an extremely dangerous takedown and figured a few more eyeballs on the plan couldn't hurt. The only suggestion Tomasovic had was to place a couple of SWAT vehicles he'd loaned the narcs at a nearby fire station for quick access.

Erin was covering the surveillance around the clock now. She'd decided that even if the grocery store was closed the crooks might be doing other activities that were related, so it was worth the extra effort. The pending robbery caused the stress level amongst the narcs to rise a little. They knew in the back of their heads that they could be smack dab in the middle of a robbery at a moment's notice. There's a psychological cost to having your self-defense engines running constantly. Cam came to work in the late afternoon so he and Erin could be around for the bulk of the stakeout coverage.

As he relieved her around the corner from the gang house, she said, "Court is killing us right now. I've had five guys working days today because of court. I didn't authorize any overtime because we're not at the three-day weekend yet, but you might need to call out someone if I can't find you some help."

Cam nodded, "Okay, go beat the brush and see who's available." He'd noticed Erin had her guitar setting beside her. "Serenading the Nortenos on your code 5?"

Erin said, "Randal here, has been my partner lately, so I thought music was better than listening to non-stop ideas about insane inventions." Randy acted insulted.

Erin returned to the squad room and looked over the duty chart. Everyone was either in court, on days off, or busy on other details. Randy had already put in a twelve-hour shift. She was about to call someone in from their days off when Terrence walked through the squad room.

"T-man, what brings you over here?"

"Hi Erin, I just needed to get a copy of Tommy's report on our meth arrest. We've got a court hearing coming up."

"Terrence, I've got to find someone to babysit Cam for a few hours on our 211 code 5. Don't suppose you need a little OT?"

"Ya, I could do that. Josephine's out of town at her sister's and I could use departmental time to read this report and finish a couple others. Is my uniform okay, or do I need to change? I didn't bring civvies with me today."

"Hang on." Erin called Cam and asked.

"Tell him to snag Todd's trench coat hanging by the door. That will cover his uniform enough to get by in a car."

Erin told Terrence what Cam said and had him to take his personal car to the stakeout, then he could just drive home from there.

Terrence walked up to Cam's UC car and Cam hit the unlock button. As Terrence sat down, he set a thermos of coffee and a bag of chocolate chip cookies on the center console.

"Josephine keeps telling me I got to lose some weight and then she keeps baking me cookies. Woman's trying to drive me insane."

Cam laughed and said, "Here, let me help you with that problem." He grabbed a couple cookies out of the bag. Terrence poured them some coffee.

Terrence asked, "So, how's the new baby and the pregnant lady?"

"All is well. The baby's a sweetheart. I think she's already a daddy's girl. She lights up when she sees me. Jane's as big as a sumo wrestler. I kid her about looking like one of those nature channel shots of a snake that ate a pig. She's thin and has a huge belly."

Terrence laughed and shook his head. "Boy you're in dangerous territory messing with a pregnant woman."

"So, Cam, what's going on here?"

"We got Ortiz and one other guy inside right now. The other guy came over about an hour ago. He was carrying a big gym bag which could mean something. I'm not sure what, but something."

Terrence grunted, "Well, we'll just stand-by to stand-by." They had their coffee and cookies and waited.

Cam thought he'd work on Terrence just a little. "Hey Terrence, want to hear everything I like about being a Sergeant?"

"No."

Cam ignored Terrence and began to explain every advantage to being a Sergeant.

Just as Terrence thought he might have to use a crude word to get Cam to shut his mouth the crook's front door opened.

Cam brought up his field glasses and said, "We got Ortiz and his number one buddy heading to the car. We'll follow them and I guess we'll just leave the house uncovered. They're the important ones."

Terrence said, "Sounds right."

As they followed Ortiz from a healthy distance Cam recognized his route of travel. "I think he's headed to the pawn shop on Story Road. Let's see if we can find a good place to hide this car so they won't get spooked."

Terrence said, "How about behind that building on the right? There are a couple of old plastic chairs for employee breaks. We'll look like we work there."

"I swear to Buddha, Terrence, you're smart enough to be a Sergeant. Button up the coat so your uniform doesn't show."

Terrence said, "You keep nagging me and I'll think you're applying for a job as my wife."

Cam and Terrence sat in the chairs and sipped coffee like they belonged there and Cam kept an eye on the store. Every few minutes he'd sneak a look through his field glasses and when he panned the surrounding area, he saw another vehicle with two older males watching the store.

He handed the glasses to Terrence, "Tell me what you see in that pickup truck."

Terrence spotted the older model Silverado and studied it a while. "They're too old to be cops. At first, I figure they might be ATF watching for straw sales, but I don't think so. The driver's got to be 70."

Cam added, "A moment ago I saw them spotting the place with a pair of field glasses."

Terrence lowered the glasses and said, "Man, this is weird. I wish I could eyeball those dudes. They dropped the tailgate on the truck to hide the rear plate and the front is up against that bush. I don't think that's an accident. You don't think they're casing the place to stick it up, do you?"

Cam shrugged, "Anything's possible."

Terrence said, "Cam, I got me an idea unless you got a plan."

"Nope, I'm drawing a blank."

Terrence said, "Give me them cookies and I'll be right back."

Terrence got out of the chair and walked away from the street, north on Story Road. Cam had no idea what he was up to and why it would require cookies. About five minutes later a homeless woman walked past Cam's car toward the pickup. She'd stop and examine garbage on the road side and stuffed one empty can into the shopping cart she pulled behind her. She walked over to the pickup and looked in all the windows. As Cam was trying to figure out what was happening Terrence sat back down in the plastic chair.

"That crazy old lady is Sonia, she's one of the smartest nut jobs on my beat and she'll do damn near anything for one of Josephine's cookies. She's wearing my body camera and I told her I need pictures of the truck plates and the guy's faces. I couldn't do that with most of my street folks. They'd run off and sell the camera."

Cam started smiling as he watched Sonia panhandle at both windows. Through his field glasses he saw the driver hand her some money and shoo her away. She slowly walked back in the direction she came from, taking her time to inspect imagined treasures. After she was out of sight Terrence got up to go find her.

Cam waited for a few minutes and saw Ortiz leave the store. His partner was carrying a heavy gym bag and to Cam's surprise he had Ortiz pop the hood. He then placed the bag into the engine compartment and it looked like he was tying it to something before they closed the hood and drove away. Cam walked back to his car impressed with the crook's creativity. Cops will look in trunks, but they seldom have suspects pop the hood. When they were out of sight, he started the car and went to snag Terrence. He was a half block away when Cam drove up beside him. Terrence jumped into the car with his body camera in his hand.

Cam said, "The crooks just left and I'll bet they're en route home with a bag full of guns. So, did she get us some pictures?"

"I think so, but you'll have to view this thing when you get back to the station. She also got six bucks from those guys. They wanted her gone big time. She'll be drinking wine and eating cookies all night long."

Cam was right. They intercepted Ortiz quickly. It isn't smart for a parolee to drive around with guns in his car, so he headed straight home. Terrence and Cam couldn't wait to get access to Sonia's video.

CHAPTER 28

Cynthia Spencer was enraged and devastated all at once. A small, shy freshman at San Jose State University had gone to the "Hot Spot" with some friends several months ago. She was under age, but one of her older girl friends bought her a couple of drinks. As the evening and drinking progressed her friends got side tracked by some cute boys and Amber Campbell met Brian Defoe. Five months later her family and friends would see her pictures on a porn site. Her face was obscured, but the tattoo of a turquoise dolphin jumping over a yellow moon on her hip was unmistakable. The pictures were debasingly crude and graphic and the only way she could live with this humiliation and shame was to not live. Being a diabetic she knew what a massive dose of insulin would do, so she did it.

Cynthia told the whole story of the rape of Amber and her death on the website and created a log of the two rapists' daily activities hour-by-hour, in case anybody needed to know where they were. The battle of the lawyers began, each threatening the other with lawsuits and blaming violence and death on the other's actions. The women of the support group just wanted the suspects to die.

∞

Cam needed to talk with Lieutenant Glen. He was generally comfortable breaking rules, but this Ortiz robbery plan was breaking new ground in the game of rule breaking.

He stuck his head inside Glen's office door, "Lieutenant, you got a minute?"

"Sure, come on in." Cam shut the door.

"Oh, a closed-door minute, is it?" Cam shrugged.

"What's up, Sergeant?"

"Well, two things. I need you to access the cloud and view Terrence's body cam footage. He stuck it on a homeless lady and had her video a pickup truck with two occupants. They were staking out the pawn shop where Ortiz was buying guns last night. I checked with other law enforcement and ATF, it doesn't appear they were cops." Cam handed the camera to Glen.

"How did she wear this thing without the people in the car noticing?"

Cam laughed, "Terrence stuck it in the bottom of a bag of his wife's cookies. He ripped a little hole in the bag for the camera lens and told her not to be too obvious about showing the car occupants the bag. It worked because they just told her to go away and handed her six bucks."

Glen laughed, "Well we'll see what she got. It might be some swell close-up pictures of cookies."

Cam agreed.

"Okay, what's your other problem?"

Cam explained about the suspected purchase of guns by Ortiz. "I was giving serious thought to stopping Ortiz right there at the pawn shop with a marked unit and arresting him for the guns. His parole status would have let me search him and Danny Dominquez would have violated him on the spot. The guns would have sent him back for a couple of years. I could still do the search at his house. It might be better than waiting for the robbery to go down. Shit could get out of control."

Glen leaned back in his chair, rubbed his mustache and goatee with the palm of his hand in a downward stoke several times.

"I liked it better when you did crap like this on your own and told me about it later." Cam wasn't sure what to say.

"Okay Cam, here's the situation. Your probable cause to search Ortiz is thin. We don't know those were guns and you've never seen any guns, so right now its informed speculation, just like your robbery prediction. Speculation based on speculation. We'll keep moving with your original plan till we have more information." Cam nodded and stood up to leave. Glen added, "Just be sure that no civilians are in the line of fire on D-Day." Cam nodded and walked out. Cam wondered about Glen's logic: Was it conveniently contrived or was he thinking like a defense attorney? One thing was for sure, no other administrator in the police department would have made that call. They all, would have gone the safe route.

∞

Betty's support group appearance was becoming problematic. She was treated kindly by the women, but she could tell they were guarding their comments when she was present. She was sure it was because she'd admonished the women against taking any vigilante action. She'd gone so far as to warn them about her responsibility to notify law enforcement if someone was threatening violence. That had dried up the counseling appointments. This group of women was different. They were angry and were prone to action rather than self-pity. She concluded that this new generation was different. Maybe the second phase of "Me Too," was "Fuck you."

∞

Juan Ortiz was a happy man. Everything was coming together just as he had planned. There weren't going to be any fuck-ups like the last time. This time he'd covered all the bases. The guns he got from the pawn shop were all cold with no traceable owners. The guy he bought them from told him they came from garage sales or gun shows. Any registration was to false owners that couldn't be found. He was even going to have surveillance on the store before he pulled the stick-up to make sure the cops weren't watching the place. He had it all covered. He'd be famous and respected by the gang.

Glen had the body camera footage accessed from the cloud and viewed it repeatedly. He asked the tech assistant to print several hard copy photo stills and had a copy of the download logged into evidence.

As he walked back to his office, he tried to plan his next step. This was a huge problem that was going to have far-reaching ramifications. Just when he thought he had the Sanchez complaint tamped down this ugly bitch reared its head.

He sat at his desk, looked at the photos and said to them, "Shit, shit, shit!"

Lieutenant Glen was allowed to set his own work hours. He did keep a schedule posted with his secretary so the administration and his narcs knew where to find him, but it allowed him the flexibility to make staff meetings and keep an eye on his troops. Lately he'd been working a lot of days because it was the time of year when they held staff meetings related to the budget and yearly planning. He needed to fix that, because all the meetings were driving him crazy, not to mention that things on the narc squad were getting volatile.

Glen walked into the narc squad weekly supervisors' meeting and pulled up a chair. "Go ahead, I've got a few things to cover when you're done."

Erin, Jesse and Bobby waited for Cam to explain the week's priorities. "Okay, so Erin's roofie case is on hold till trial time. Bobby's plan for the Juan Ortiz 211 is in place and we're keeping the surveillance around the clock except a few hours in the early morning. The only loose end there is the guys in the pickup code 5-ing the place along with us." Cam looked at Lieutenant Glen.

Glen nodded, "I'll get to that in a minute. Go ahead with anything else you've got."

Cam asked, "Gentlemen, lady?"

Erin spoke up, "Betty Ward and I talked about the support group she's meeting with for the roofie rape victims. She reports some bad ju ju. She thinks someone is going to do something nasty beyond the petty vandalism we've been seeing. She can't put any detail to her feeling, but I respect her judgement."

Jesse shrugged, "Not much we can do beyond what we've already done. We warned them, talked to their attorneys and Betty warned them. Sometimes you catch the wave and sometimes it catches you."

Cam smiled, "Anybody else?"

Jesse added, "I got an attorney taking coke and sex for his fee. A gal I busted for sales and possession of coke contacted me and asked if I could work out a sentence reduction if she does her own attorney. She really hates the guy and I guess she doesn't have much confidence in a coke-head lawyer."

Everyone laughed, Jesse continued, "Randy and I have a plan to catch him red handed or red nosed. I'll tell you guys all about it when I get the details worked out."

Cam pointed at Glen, "Lieutenant."

Glen cleared his throat, "This rape investigation has taken a dangerous twist. Cam and Terrence had a video made by putting a body camera on a homeless lady and recording a pickup truck doing surveillance on the pawn shop that Ortiz was using. I just got the download and the old lady did a good job recording the occupants of the truck." Glen pulled out a dozen large, grainy pictures of two men and a license plate and slid them across the table for the crew to examine. "This truck comes back registered to Carl Blake a friend of Tony Spencer, Cynthia Spencer's father. He's a retired cop, that I worked with years ago. If he's watching a gun dealer who sells cold weapons it's fair to assume, he doesn't want a gun that can be traced. I know this guy and he's old school. He's not afraid of taking action, and on top of that he's smart. If he does something, he'll do it right."

Everyone was quiet till Cam said, "Swell, this thing could affect the whole department. Now we have two cops involved. I can just see the headlines, Police Assassination Squad."

Glen nodded, "So, what options do we have?"

Bobby said, "If we warn him off, we tip our hand and it's probably pointless."

Jesse added, "If we arrest the pawn shop gun dealer and twist him, he might give us the name of his customers, but I'm guessing we don't have proof of him selling and his customers won't talk, so he'll lawyer up if he's smart. Plus, if we pop him now, we blow the robbery case. Ortiz will get wind of it and retool his plans."

Erin asked, "So, what's Spencer's and Blake's plan? To off the rapists, then dispose or just dump the gun?"

Glen nodded, "That would be my guess. I'm assuming Carl Blake got word of this gun dealer through some old contacts when he worked vice and was just seeing how the operation worked the night you guys saw him. He'll probably score a gun later or he may have already bought one. Any leaks about this will create a huge headache for this investigation and anything attached to it. Let's think about this for a while. It's one more example of speculation based on speculation. We really don't have any actionable facts. We didn't see anybody do anything illegal and we didn't see any guns. I hesitated to open this can of worms, but I figure for officer safety reasons, you guys needed to know."

Everyone nodded.

Glen got up to leave and said, "I'll be around a little more the next few weeks. Let's keep on this thing and see how it breaks."

One of the famous quotes about law enforcement is, "Police work is hours of butt numbing boredom punctuated by moments of sheer terror." For narcs it just a different version of the same thing. You wade through typical buy cases and search warrants, then get the case where all hell breaks loose. The narc squad should have seen this coming.

Parole officer Danny Dominquez called Cam on his cell the Friday before the upcoming three-day weekend. "Cam, I just did my normal home visit of Juan Ortiz and he was so damned nervous he could barely contain himself. He was overly polite and the parole agent I took with me said he'd bet money that guy's gonna pull some shit real soon, and I never told the other agent about your suspicion of a robbery. I'm telling you man, he's ready to blow."

Cam said, "Ya, my guys on the stakeout said they think it's going down earlier than we thought based on all the activity. We've stepped up the number of officers on site and taken a few preliminary steps here to get ready."

Danny was having guilt pangs about how this was going down. "I feel like I should either bust Ortiz now or come work with you guys on this. Both options suck. I either fuck up a case for you or get myself in big trouble."

Cam gritted his teeth. All he needed was for Dominquez to get a guilty conscience and blow this operation. "How about this Danny, when I think it's about to go down and can really use parole's help, I call you and you meet us at the store. That way when you do your report, you can just start with, I was called by Sergeant Michaelson on this date and time and told one of my parolees was involved in a robbery. So, you can help us, but not get in hot water for sitting on the information."

"Ya, that sounds good. That will work. I'll stand by till I hear from you and I'm guessing it will be soon. And Cam, he's a dangerous asshole."

"Got it Danny. Thanks."

Cam let Lieutenant Glen know about the call and Glen told him that he needed to set his operation in motion. Glen warned Cam that the crooks will likely have counter surveillance and that Cam should layer his response. First undercover officers trying to spot the crooks' surveillance then the robbery responding officer, then SWAT if possible. Everything had to go down with precision timing. The perimeter undercover people had to get citizens to a safe retreat and not blow the robbery response officers. A lot of other law enforcement people had to be notified confidentially, so they didn't accidentally go to the store. There would be a lot of logistics to this operation.

CHAPTER 29

Juan Ortiz decided to change the timing of this rip off. Monday was too late. An excon he knew was talking with Juan and explained that the armored car pickups didn't take the holiday off and if he waited till Monday the big take would be gone. Juan decided that Sunday morning would be the perfect time. Everyone would have done their shopping Saturday in preparation for the big game Sunday and if he hit it when the store opened Sunday morning early there would be a lot of cash on hand. He'd run surveillance on the store and found out the money truck arrived about 10:00 am. He'd hit the place at 9:00.

∞

Bobby was coordinating the various stages of the 211 operation. He had Erin set up the surveillance of the parking lot where the Safeway was located. She used Anna from her patrol shift and herself to be undercover shoppers. They dressed like ladies shopping for groceries and even had child car seats in their undercover units. She also used a reserve officer the squad occasional employed because of his baby face. Eddie Angle was 19 but looked 16. Then there was an older Vice Sergeant that liked overtime, Earl Yoki was 55 but looked 65 with a scraggly beard and a pot belly. He looked like he'd just crawled out of his fishing boat. Their job was to rotate in and out of the parking lot to spot counter surveillance. When the actual robbery went down, they would be the ones that cleared citizens away from a potential shootout.

Bobby then moved to the actual take down teams. He'd contacted SWAT and Lieutenant Tomasovic put some people on standby, but without an exact time he couldn't dedicate officers to the narc team. They had too many other obligations like warrant services and calls from patrol.

Bobby was able to use the vehicles Tomasovic loaned him, so he placed them in hidden locations near the scene. Narcs could use the heavily armored vans to block the crooks' exit and they made good cover in the event there was a shootout. Todd and Jessy got qualified on the M4 rifle, so they would be assigned to each crook vehicle along with an officer armed with a shotgun. They could be used to blow windows and tires safely without rounds traveling hundreds of yards. Bobby also had Randy equip both teams with the tire clamps he'd purchased. Randy instructed the teams on how to apply them. Once they were in place the car was going nowhere.

The undercover officers on site would hopefully see the crooks arrive and that would set everything in motion, but Cam was relying on the stakeout officers watching Juan Ortiz's gang house to be the real tripwire. The squad was rotating officers through the observation post up till about three days ago, then Cam and his crew figured it would become too dangerous to have people in a car watching the place. The crooks were just too paranoid and there wasn't a good place to hide. They opted for a surveillance camera mounted in an old broken-down Chrysler sedan. A camera was rigged into the head lamp, powered by the car's battery. It sent a picture of the front of Ortiz's home to a computer link very much like a doorbell camera. It could be watched in the Sergeant's office or on a couple different cell phones. Bobby found the current cell phone addiction phenomenon useful. He could have a couple of shoppers viewing the site while walking around the grocery store parking lot or into the store itself and it would look perfectly normal. It also recorded the footage, so it could be backed up for reviewing and potentially for court.

Sunday morning at 8:30 Anna and Earl were put on alert. They were sitting together at a donut shop located at the North end of the shopping center parking lot. Earl was eating a cinnamon roll the size of a car tire and Anna was nursing a cup of coffee.

Bobby hit them on a tactical net hard for citizens to unscramble, "Anna, N3."

"Go ahead N3."

"Status?"

"Watch Earl inhale 12,000 calories."

Bobby smiled, "We got movement on our end. Expect company."

Anna keyed her mic, "Ya, we been watching the live feed. Looks like two-in-one ride."

"Affirmative, let us know when they arrive and their position."

"10-4."

Anna told Earl, "Looks like you've got more work to do on your pending heart attack, so I'll walk to the other side of the parking lot. That way we'll have both sides covered."

As she got up from the table Earl said, "Don't forget your nine-dollar coffee. Looks like you still have three dollars left in that cup." Anna gave Earl a big fake smile and walked slowly to the other side of the lot along the store fronts.

About twenty minutes later a lowered Honda with two Hispanic males pulled into the parking lot. They parked in front of the store and remained in the car. Anna slowly walked far behind them across the lot to rejoin Earl.

As Anna sat across from Earl she said, "Looks like our two friends are just gunna watch from their car."

"Yep, real fucking geniuses. Why don't you call Bobby? Someone's gonna need to take them down when it's bust time."

Anna hit Bobby on the radio and explained things. "Okay, Anna, when the arrest team starts their run you and Earl take down those two schmucks unless you hear different."

"Okay, the drivers' on the phone right now, so I'm guessing it's to give the all clear."

Anna told Earl, "We're to take them down when it happens. Any ideas, Sergeant?"

Earl thought a moment. "The problem is that open area where they're parked. If they're paying attention, they'll see us walking up behind them. They might leave before it goes down. They might be part of the crew, but I'm guessing they're just backup in case something goes wrong." Anna agreed.

"Okay, Anna, how bout you take off that sweatshirt and put your hair up in one of those lady jock pony tails and wiggly your assets in front of those boys' car, while I sneak up behind them and get a gun screwed in their ear?" Earl gave Anna back a big fake smile.

She shook her head, "You've been working vice too long Earl. You're beginning to think like your clientele."

"True, and these boys are my clientele. I guarantee, they'll be watching you like a hawk."

Anna didn't like this plan, but was drawing a blank on other ideas, "Okay, we'll do it your way, but only because I can't think of a better one."

Anna rummaged around in her purse for a hair tie as Earl got up. He said, "Guess I'll pee while I can. Don't eat the rest of my cinnamon roll."

Bobby alerted the troops that two vehicles had pulled up to Ortiz's location and parked toward the side of the house. These cars hadn't been seen before, so Bobby assumed they were freshly stolen vehicles that crooks often used to pull 211 jobs.

Glen and Cam were standing behind Bobby watching him coordinate the operation. They both out ranked him, but felt he had a better grasp on the people involved and logistics, so they let him run things.

He turned around to face them, "I'm going to move the two arrest teams into position and notify everyone about Anna's two crooks. Cam, do you want to get Danny Dominquez moving?"

Cam said, "Sure."

"And Lieutenant, what about Tomasovic's people?"

Glen said, "I don't know if there's time, but we can try. Give me a staging area for them."

Bobby had a city map of the location and was looking it over. "I think we can get them pretty close because Tommy's been cruising the area and hasn't found any mobile counter surveillance."

Everyone was making phone calls and positioning themselves to make it all work smoothly. What everyone knew in the back of their heads was that most battle plans are rewritten in the first five minutes of an encounter. Things never go as planned.

∞

Juan Ortiz was on a high that was right up there with the first time he snorted meth. He was pacing and talking non-stop. He was yelling instructions to his crew and checking his weapons repeatedly. He went over details with both of his two-man crews. He'd decided that he'd add one more man so he could cover both entrances and have two men to clean out the cash registers while he forced the manager to open the safe. All his excitement was contagious, and his crew was getting hyped. Deep down they were afraid, but knew all scary things required a leap of faith.

As he loaded his crew into the two cars, he told a remaining older gang member, "You make the calls when I tell you." He and the gang headed out.

∞

Bobby had all of his people in place and waiting. The tension was high, but unlike Ortiz and his crew the narc squad got quiet when they were nervous. They reviewed tactics and procedures and tried to think of anything they missed.

About ten minutes after Bobby notified everyone that two cars left Ortiz's gang house the department received a call of a fire at a senior citizens' home across town. The citizen reporting the fire claimed there were dozens of elderly people that needed to be moved. Fire and police were dispatched.

Ortiz had set his operation in motion. The gang member he left at the house made the call for two of his men to throw flares into dry grass and trash behind the rest home. They also threw several mason jars full of gasoline which ignited a wooden fence. Then they made the 911 call.

∞

Cam looked at Bobby, "Diversion call?"

Bobby shrugged, "If it is, it doesn't affect us. Narcs don't handle stuff like that, but it would bleed off a patrol response to the robbery."

Glen returned, "Tomasovic is going to try to break away one tactical unit that's serving a search warrant to help us. I told him the staging area to hold at, and gave him our radio channel, so he could monitor the timing."

Bobby stood up and said to Glen and Cam, "I can run this from the field and I think it's time for us to 11-98 with our teams. Cam, you and I are hooking up with Terrence and Todd. Lieutenant, you're with Jesse, Al and Randy. Tommy's in a mobile unit to go where he's needed. Erin, Anna, Earl and the reserve Eddie are on foot. I hope I've covered everything."

Lieutenant Glen said, "Well, if you've missed something it escapes me too."

Everybody met up with their teams and waited for the word from Bobby. They had to be careful and not jump the gun. They'd scare everybody off if they did. They also had to make sure they weren't visible when the crooks ran out of the store, or they'd run back inside and create a hostage situation.

"N3, code 5." (Earl and Anna didn't have a real N number.)

Bobby answered, "Go ahead Earl."

"They just arrived and positioned the two vehicles in the lot approximately in front of the entrance doors. Three crooks in one, two in the other. Ready to copy vehicle descriptions?"

"Go ahead." After Earl described the two gang cars, Bobby said, "Units copy?" He received a series of double clicks signaling the other car heard the description.

Three minutes later, after Ortiz set his phone down, the crooks exited the car. They had on full face masks of assorted celebrities and a couple wore long trench coats hiding long-barrel weapons.

Earl hit the air: "N3 and all units, our boys have exited their cars wearing masks and carrying something under their coats. They're about to enter the store."

Bobby was amazed at how laid-back Earl's voice was. It sounded like he was ordering an ice cream flavor and selecting his toppings. "All units, get to your final approach positions."

The two takedown cars full off narcs moved toward their designated positions at the side of the building where they'd be out of sight of the crooks when they exited, but close enough to move in fast.

All the foot officers, Erin and Eddie started to walk slowly toward the store so they could steer civilians away when the crooks entered their cars.

Earl had a new, unexpected problem: what to do with the two counter surveillance suspects. "N3, Earl."

"Go ahead."

"Problem Bobby. If we leave those two surveillance bangers till it's bust time, they might get in behind our people and they'll see us putting on the tire clamps. They'll probably start moving when the others exit the doors. I recommend Anna and I do it now, and hope we can get out of sight before they exit. Robberies take a few minutes."

Bobby looked at Cam, "Crap, what do you think?" Cam thought a few seconds. Earl waited, thinking, "time matters here guys." Glen waited, knowing what he would order done.

Cam nodded an affirmation.

Bobby keyed his mic, "Do it."

Earl looked at Anna, "Okay, kiddo, we're up. When you hear me yell at those schmucks, you take the window I'm not at." Anna started to walk toward the crook's car. Earl said, "And Anna, don't forget to sell it, you're hot and you know it. My safe approach depends on your sex appeal. If you're a dud, I'm in trouble."

Anna was used to danger. She'd been a cop a long time and handled her share of hot calls, but these crazy vice and narcotics cops took things to a whole new level. So much of what they did was hanging it out there all by yourself.

All she could think to say was, "Right…"

As Anna approached the crook's car she started to get pissed at that sexist, dinosaur, pig, Sergeant Earl Yoki. Leave it to a vice cop to pimp out a fellow female cop. She decided that if she was going to do this then, by god, she was going to do it right. She was wearing a blue pair of baggy hiking shorts. She turned down two folds of the waist band which pulled the shorts up tight. Then folded up the cuff once, which made them short shorts. Her next move was to tuck her tank top into her shorts as tight as she could and since Anna was a naturally gifted women, with the strap of her purse running across the front of her chest, she would be noticed. As she started her approach with a sway that was hard to miss, she thought, "Well if I ever get fired as a cop, maybe I'll qualify to be a pole dancer."

It worked. One of the crooks said something to his buddy and they were both laughing and taking it all in. They weren't looking in the rear-view mirror. The passenger in the crook's car rolled down the window to say something to Anna when Earl, seeing his break, ran quietly across the open parking lot to the crook's window and shoved his snub-nosed revolver in the guy's face.

Anna heard Earl yell, "Police! Hands up! Get your Goddamn hands on your head!" Anna was about to go to the driver's side when she saw Tommy jerk the driver's door open with his left hand and screw his Glock into the crook's ear. She'd forgotten all about Tommy. He'd been monitoring the conversation between Earl and Bobby and figured he could help move this thing along faster, so the crooks in the store wouldn't see it go down.

Tommy grabbed the crook by his shirt and pulled him out of the car onto his face. He jumped on his back and put cuffs on him.

He said to Anna, "Help Earl cuff his guy and we'll lay them in the back till this is over."

Anna ran around and helped Earl cuff his crook. They laid one on the back seat and the other on the floor, then Earl got in and sat on the edge of the seat.

He said, "I got these dip-shits. I'll just lay down when the crooks come out. You two start walking around and keep people safe." Anna and Tommy both nodded. After all, Earl was a Sergeant. Earl, smiling, added "And Anna, fix yourself, you look like a hooker."

Anna was headed back to kick Earl's ass when Tommy grabbed her arm. As she stopped Tommy looked her up and down and wiggled his eyebrows. She backhanded him across the chest.

When the crooks entered the store from two different doors, they blocked the exits with a long string of shopping carts. Ortiz had an AR15 and one other crook had a shotgun. Everyone else had semi-automatic handguns. Ortiz screamed that it was a robbery as he fired a burst from his weapon into the ceiling. He had the terrified shoppers sit down on the floor. Two crooks stood watch where they could see the doors and two crooks emptied the cash register drawers. Ortiz identified the manager and grabbed him by the hair, hauling him to the safe. As he screamed at the manager to open the safe, he slammed the guy's head into the metal door. The manager pulled out the safe key and put it into the lock, but when Ortiz couldn't open it, the manager pointed to the sign on the front of the safe saying, "This Safe Requires Two Keys. One in Possession of The Manager and The Other in Possession of The Armored Transport Carrier."

The manager said, "I'd open it for you if I could. I don't have the other key." He hid his head with both arms and squatted to the floor waiting to be shot. Ortiz put the gun to his head and thought it over. He decided it would solve nothing, so he butt stroked the manager across the head with the rifle and left with all his men. As Ortiz left the front door, he looked for his outside crew. They were supposed to give him cover fire if the cops showed up. He saw their car, but they were not in it. He assumed they had taken up a cover position somewhere in the parking lot. Both groups of crooks got in their respective cars, which they'd left facing out of the parking places and started them. When they slapped them into drive and hit the gas nothing happened. Randy's tire clamps had been attached to both cars' rear tires. That's when Ortiz began to realize that things were not what they seemed. Two tactical vehicles pulled into position with a fortified side of the SWAT vehicle facing the crooks. The officers bailed out the safe side and took up a position behind their vehicle.

Ortiz was in a full-blown rage, "Pedro, move this fucking car. Drive, man!"

Pedro answered, "It don't go, man, something wrong," as police loudspeakers in the background said, "This is the Police Department. Occupants of the car, get your hands on your head, now!"

Ortiz wasn't going down without a fight. He was not going back to prison and didn't care if he died. He'd at least take some of these fucking pigs with him.

Ortiz looked at his men and screamed, "Come on, shoot some fucking-body," as he kicked open his front passenger door. Ortiz started pulling the trigger as his weapons barrel extended through the door. Three rounds hit an adjacent parked car before Todd ripped Ortiz with two three-round bursts from his M14.

Terrence dumped two rounds of .00 buck through the front window of the suspect's car and waited to assess the damage, mostly because he saw Cam, out of the corner of his eye, put a hand on Todd's shoulder and say, "Hold, Todd."

The crook's car became strangely quiet and Cam noticed a leg sticking out of the front passenger door. It had a steady flow of blood running down it and flowing over the sock and shoe. Whoever was bleeding that much would die. Cam had little doubt about that.

Cam yelled again, "Police. Get your hands, on top of your head!"

One man inside the car complied with Cam's instructions. The other two could not. They were dead. Todd's .223 rounds opened up three major wounds in Juan Ortiz. The round that caught his femoral leg artery was the most serious. He bled out in a few seconds. The other dead gang member didn't even look like he'd been shot. A .00-buck round from Terrence's shotgun deflected off a chrome head rest bar and traveled through the gang member's right eye. The pellet didn't exit, it just seemed to bounce around inside the skull.

While all this was going down Erin, Anna, Tommy and Eddie were badging citizens and giving them simple instructions to make them safe. They were usually told, "There's a gun battle in the parking lot. Please go into a store until it's over."

While Ortiz was making his last stand, Lieutenant Glen, Jesse, Al and Randy were in position on the other robbery suspects' vehicle. Jesse had just made his announcement of, "Police. Get your hands on your head!" when a fully armored SWAT tactical vehicle rolled into the other side of the crook's car. The tactical tank intentionally rammed the rear end of the crook's vehicle, causing it to jump a foot into the air because the tire clamp wouldn't let it roll on its wheels.

The SWAT loudspeaker said, in an almost bored voice, "Surrender now or we'll open fire." The two occupants immediately surrendered.

Marked units were called in for prisoner transport as well as detective division to handle the officer-involved shooting report. The store manager refused an ambulance, but was being attended to by EMT's.

Tommy and Anna went back to help Earl with his two prisoners and found Earl had thrown one crook on top of the other one that was lying on the floor and was sitting on them.

As the squad members stood around accessing the damage and assigning jobs to various officers, Cam looked at the crew and said, "Erin, why don't you Eddie, Earl, Anna and Tommy go back to the gang house and serve the search warrant. I'll be over when I get things coordinated here." She nodded and started to leave.

The Lieutenant said, "Erin, let me go talk with SWAT. I'll have them make entry for you as long as they're here."

Erin smiled, "I like it when the Lieutenant works with us. SWAT teams follow you around."

Randy said, "No shit. They just ram people and everyone behaves."

Danny Dominquez walked up to Cam, "Well, I guess my work here is done. None of these other clowns belongs to me and I'll just close out Mr. Ortiz's file."

Cam shrugged, "Oh well."

After all the warrants were served and evidence was seized the gang's future looked bad. Everyone went to jail for serious charges. Even the members at the house were arrested for conspiracy to commit robbery because they were in on the execution of it. They had made phone calls and used arson to further a crime. The house was full of evidence of the robbery. They had maps and handwritten plans made by Ortiz. A runaway juvenile girl at the house was cooperating with detectives and had implicated the gang in dozens of crimes, not to mention all the weapons found in the home and all three vehicles at the scene.

From a prosecution point of view, it was a very successful investigation. Lieutenant Glen sat in on the squad's supervisor meeting the next week because he wanted to discuss a few things.

Glen started, "Alright you magnificent warriors, what's the collective opinion on our parolee surveillance operation?"

No one wanted to go first, but Cam figured since he was the lead investigator and supervisor, he was obligated to say something. "It bagged a lot of bad guys and damage to civilians was light, but it could have been ugly. According to witness accounts of the robbery, Ortiz almost killed the manager. It was a close call. We had civilians hiding all over the store. That causes me to second guess my decision to allow it to go down. Maybe we should have taken them off earlier."

Glen waited for others to comment.

Erin said, "This is not unlike the decoy operation we were doing on reverse buys. The potential benefits may not be worth the risks."

Bobby looked at Erin and nodded, "I agree, but never say never. There are some situations where letting a crime go down is justified. I think we have to call each one individually."

Jesse added, "I think the parolee surveillance tactic has some value. It's a good slack time activity for our narcs. Remember, we still have two parolees being watched on our computer prediction program. Danny Dominquez and other parole agents can keep us updated on the current dangerous crooks, we just need to be a little more cautious about when we take them down."

Glen liked what he was hearing. These were solid supervisors that didn't let the hunt override their ethical obligations. This was the growth he and Captain Jenkins were looking for. Cam was a creative and bold cop, but his recklessness scared everyone. Glen's belief was that people like Cam were like sailboats, you didn't fight the wind, you harnessed it.

"Okay Cam, what else do we have going on?"

"The old timers and the pawn shop surveillance. Erin's been following up on that because it's tied to her rape case."

Erin updated everyone with her latest information. "I set up a little surveillance on the two guys who were pictured in front of our gun dealer. Nothing serious, but I'm having some of the guys drive by their homes and record plates to see where Tony Spencer and Carl Blake spend their time. When I was talking with Al about this stuff Earl Yoki overheard us. He said these guys were part of a group of retire cops who have breakfast most mornings at a local diner. Apparently, some of these guys are freshly retired and some are years out. There's nine or ten of them."

Jesse said, "Their meeting could be harmless or it could be a conspiracy."

Bobby added, "This could just be a normal social gathering, but the gun stakeout changes everything."

Glen nodded, "I talked with Tony Spencer already and I see no benefit in repeating myself. I guess we're in a wait-and-see mode as far as these two guys. I do think we could probably start some investigative work here. Any ideas?"

Cam spoke up, "We need to interview the gun shop about the robbery. There might be a way to ask about their other customers. I don't think we'll get much out of them, but we should try."

Erin added, "I need to look at this group of cops a little closer and see if there are any patterns or prior unusual activities."

Glen pushed back his chair and leaned forward putting his elbows on his knees, "Anything else?"

Jesse said, "I'm still working on my coke snorting lawyer, but it's a few days out."

Glen stood up, "Alright, keep those reports coming. Some of your squad have a few outstanding." Everyone went back to work.

CHAPTER 30

Tony Spencer and his retired buddies generally just joked and laughed their way through breakfast, but lately things had become serious. They always met at the same place they used when they were cops. Angie's Diner, was an out-of-the-way restaurant that allowed them to have private conversations and didn't rush them if they sat for a couple of hours. They always started early because, like most retired folk, they went to bed early and got up early. All the regulars were there and had finished their breakfast by 7:00. Tony Spencer made an announcement during a lull in the conversation.

"Alright, gentlemen, I think we need to convene the 10-35 club." 10-35 was police code for confidential information. When the radio desk wanted to let a beat cop know secretly, that he had stopped a guy that was wanted, they asked, "Are you 10-35?" Three of the retired cops picked up their checks and said goodbye to their friends. They had a rough idea about what the remaining six men would be talking about because everyone knew about Tony's daughter, but they didn't want to be involved in any extra-legal activities, so they found it easier to leave and everyone understood. This organization had been in existence for years and had only one of its original founding members. George Codoni was pushing 85 and had been retired for decades. When he and three other retired ex-cops started this informal little group, it wasn't such a big ethical leap. In those days cops often bent the rules to get justice and their fellow officers didn't see a need to get too judgmental. It seemed like a natural extension back then to occasional do in retirement what they did while they were working. As the years went by, they realized that the world around them had changed and, more importantly, law enforcement had changed. The "L.A. Confidential," way of doing business wasn't tolerated anymore and so they had to change their behavior. Some of the officers just walked away, but George Codoni was unwilling to give up that easily. There were assholes that needed to die and the justice system had become a joke. Being an extremely effect cop in his day, he'd found a way to deal out a little justice with minimal risk. That really was the key. Fix only the problems that were truly serious and minimize the danger. Early on, George had devised ways to reduce the risk that were creative.

One step was to have only experienced cops who understood the law and conducting investigations involved, but the real stroke of genius was to have any drastic solutions executed by a member with serious medical problems. This option was not always possible, but given the age and health problems of most retired cops, it was often available. One of the earliest "accidental deaths" that really launched the club was of a child molester released on a faulty Miranda confession. The suspect admitted his guilt and the child identified him, but a very able attorney got the confession thrown out and the identification voided because it was a result from an illegal confession. The fact that the suspect had prior charges could not be used against him. George Codoni and several other breakfast buddies were outraged. One of their number, a guy named Louis who happened to have just had a very disappointing medical checkup regarding a persistent cough, arrested and cuffed the suspect using an old badge and his cuffs. He was careful to put the cuffs on loosely over the top of the suspect jacket which is almost never done because of the possibility of the suspect slipping out of them. Louis was careful to make sure they were tight enough, but not so tight as to leave marks. He'd pulled the suspect's T-shirt that had, "Kill Them All And Let God Sort Them Out," printed on the front over his head from the back, so he couldn't see. Then he took the suspect to a river park and walked him to wide spot in river where he could get down to the water across a sandy beach. He took the suspect swimming and sat on his back for a few minutes.

As he waited for the forty-year-old pervert to stop kicking he told him, "I'm going to let God sort this one out." Later he removed the cuffs, pulled the T-shirt off the guy's head and pushed the body into the main river flow. Four days later the news reports would announce a man was found fully clothed floating about two miles from the park with no signs of foul play. His sister thought it strange because he was a strong swimmer, but didn't much care because he was a major embarrassment to the family and a huge asshole. He would never molest again. That was the maiden voyage that launched the club.

Carl Blake's pancreatic cancer diagnosis was a stroke of bad luck for Carl and Brian Defoe, but good timing for Tony Spencer. Doctors told him he had about three months to live without treatment and six with treatment.

Carl laughed at the doctor, "So, you can give me an extra three months, but I have to spend it in a doctor's office and sick. No thanks." The only family he had to argue with him about that decision was a daughter who lived out of state and he hadn't told her about the cancer. Not being given to sentimentality, he figured she couldn't do anything but worry and figured it would just be easier on everybody if she was notified by the coroner's office.

George Codoni asked, "So Carl, do you have everything you need?"

"Yep, Tony and I took care of that yesterday. Now it's just a matter of timing."

George asked, "Are you feeling well enough to get it done?"

"Ya, I have some bad days, but I can manage it." What he hadn't told his buddies was that he was frequently having crippling seizures of pain that caused him to double over and throw up. He always sat down when he felt them coming, so he didn't fall over and hurt himself, but they were happening more often and with less warning. That worried him.

Tony was concerned about Carl's physical condition, but knew him to be tough as nails, "Is there going to be time to address both problems, because we can deal with the other one if you're not feeling up to it. The one thing we don't want to do is rush this operation. That's how you make mistakes."

Elden Winters, who had retired twenty years ago, said, "Do the first thing first, and then see where we are. My cardiac situation would make me a good second candidate for this operation. I don't have any immediate critical problems, but the handwriting is on the wall if you catch my drift."

Tony said, "Thanks, Elden, I'll keep that in mind. I think you're right, we should deal with the most pressing problem and worry about step two later."

The guys discussed a few other collateral issues, always being careful to talk in generalities. No one believed that one of the members of the 10-35 club would ever turn on them, but you had to be careful when you were talking about committing murder. Even the murder of predators. You never know who could be listening. They said their goodbyes and scheduled another breakfast in two days.

Carl had a cold 9mm Beretta he and Tony purchased. He had his own .357 Smith & Wesson that he preferred to use, but the Beretta was a nice weapon.

Tony and Carl had conducted a full investigation on Brian Defoe and Bradley Pope. They were helped by the website set up by the rapist's victims. They knew their daily routines and patterns and had devised a plan to hit Defoe.

Late the next evening, Carl drove his truck to a quiet residential street three blocks away from Golds Gym. He retrieved the bicycle from the back of his truck and pedaled to the rear of the gym. He was dressed in a pair of black pants and a dark blue sweatshirt with a hood. His stocking cap kept his head warm under the hood. He peeked around the corner of an adjacent warehouse and located the motion detector camera and light Tony had described to him. He was just out of activation range, so there'd be no picture of him. He pulled out a Crosman pellet pistol he'd owned for years and steadied himself against the edge of the building using it as a target support. It took him four shots to hit the camera lense and light because of the distance, but now he was free to operate without being recorded. The world was different these days. Everything was recorded. As Carl put the CO_2 pistol back in his waistband a wave of nausea and pain hit him and brought him to his knees. He didn't throw up, but he needed to rest for a couple of minutes before he could get on his bike. Maybe taking his bike was a bad idea, but he didn't want his truck near the scene. Once a powerful and effective cop, he was frustrated with how weak and tired this cancer made him.

Defoe was optimistic, all things considered. He had gotten out on bail and was still a free man. His attorney told him he had a fighting chance to beat this thing because the confession of Bradley Pope's dead little brother could be challenged. He was in love and heartbroken about his girlfriend's infidelity with Defoe. Of course, he was going to lie about it being a rape. None of the victims were able to remember anything and they were all heavy-drinking horny college girls out looking for some action. There were some tough issues to deal with, but the lawyer felt there was a possibility of success and he was pitching his defense theories to the media to hopefully plant a seed in the potential jury pool. Brian Defoe couldn't let the problems he had get him down. He needed to continue living his life. He was hitting the gym again. His looks were important to him.

CHAPTER 31

Carl had made peace with himself. He knew he was dying and was okay with it. Not that he wouldn't like to be healthy, but he had realized that living is a two-part bargain. You don't get life without death. Like a great many older people, his illnesses and age were taking their toll. He was just tired of it all. At least this final act would give it some meaning. He'd spent his whole life defending weak and victimized people. This would be a final gift to the citizens of San Jose. This guy wouldn't be around to victimize anyone else.

He prepared all day long. He laid out the clothes he would wear and tore the Beretta down to the smallest parts he could reasonably put back together. He cleaned and wiped the gun parts wearing gloves, so no fingerprints would be found. He threw away the remaining ammo from the box he used to load the gun making sure the rounds in the magazine didn't have prints. He also discarded the cleaning fluid and brushes he'd used. He placed the gun in a plastic bag to eliminate any DNA transfer.

After he completely prepared himself and his equipment he sat down and took some anti-nausea medication and some pain pills. The dull deep ache started in his stomach and radiated around to his back. The pills helped a little, but not near enough.

He knew that Defoe's workout started at 7:00 pm and would go till 9:00 pm, so he waited and watched the clock. At 8:00 pm he got in his truck and slowly drove to Golds Gym. He had plenty of time and he felt like crap. He decided that he's just drive his truck into the rear lot because the cameras were out and wouldn't record his truck or its plates, besides he didn't think he could pedal a bike tonight.

As he drove up to the back of the gym, he saw Defoe's car in the parking lot. He'd just recently gotten the vandalism repairs completed. Carl smiled because everything was on schedule. The asshole was here and would be coming out in twenty minutes. If everything went right, Carl would be home sleeping in his recliner thirty minutes later because he couldn't sleep in his bed anymore. It was just too painful on his back.

Carl slipped on a thin pair of cotton gloves and stuffed the Berretta into his sweatshirt's front pouch pocket. He kept it in a plastic bag to make sure any oils from the gun didn't touch his clothing. He walked around to the tailgate of his truck, opened it and sat down to wait.

∞

As Defoe was finishing his workout, he couldn't help but notice a cute little hard body that was doing squats next to him. She came to the gym on pretty much the same schedule as him. He had a plan that if he could get a water bottle just like hers, he could put some roofies in it, trade it with hers and help her out to her car next week when she started to get sleepy. The cops missed a small baggy of about twenty pills he had under the electronic window control switch on the car's armrest. He packed up his gym bag and thought as he was leaving the back door of the gym, that it had been a long time since he gotten laid and this little bitch looked like she was going to be a sweet ride.

∞

Carl felt like death warmed over, but he reminded himself that all he had to do was hold it together for five minutes.

The next few minutes, it all went into play. The metal door at the rear of the gym made a noise from the push bar being hit and a burst of light momentarily filled the parking lot. Carl started walking toward the exit. He had to make sure it was Defoe and that he was alone before he could do anything. Whoever the guy was he was alone and in a few more seconds Carl would know if he had the right person. Just as Defoe was getting near, Carl felt a wave of pain and nausea hit him like never before. He was trying to focus on identifying Defoe and finishing the job, but his vision was shattered by tears and the searing pain. He got closer to the guy than he liked just to be sure it was really him, but made a positive identification that it was Defoe. Carl knew the danger of taking extra time or hesitating, so he immediately pulled his gun and aimed it at Defoe. Defoe froze in his tracks like a deer in the headlights. Carl said nothing, he had only one goal which was to make the shot a clean kill. He brought the gun up to eye level and put the front sight on target right between Defoe's eyes and as he squeezed the trigger a bolt of pain hit his nervous system like lightning. He knew that accurate shooting is all about sight alignment and a smooth trigger pull, but he did what amateurs do, he jerked the trigger to try and get the round off while he was still on target. The bullet went wide missing Defoe's head by an eighth of an inch, flying over the building and landing god knows where. Carl fell to his knees and lost his grip on the gun. He was trying to find it when Defoe jumped forward and snatched it from the ground. Carl was on all his hands and knees throwing up what little stomach content he had, in a violent convulsion. As he stopped retching and leaned back on his heel's he noticed Defoe pointing the gun at his head.

"What's the problem, you pathetic old fuck? Too sick to finish the job? Let me show you how to do that. Where would you like to be shot?"

Carl recognized an amateur when he saw one. Defoe was running his mouth because his ego was in charge. Carl reached behind his back and gripped the .357 revolver that he'd carried for the first half on his law enforcement career, a trusted old friend. He punched the gun forward firing one round into Defoe's chest and then one more round into Defoe's very surprised face.

Carl knew it was a matter of seconds before someone started to investigate the gunfire, so he stood up and grabbed Defoe's gun hand and aimed it across the parking lot. He pulled the trigger firing one round from the 9mm. Then he pulled the plastic bag out of his sweatshirt pocket and placed it into Defoe's gym bag. As the back door to the gym opened, he identified himself.

"I'm an ex-cop, call the police department and tell them there's been a shooting and the cop on scene says it's code 4."

A woman in workout clothes pulled a cell phone from a waistband pocket and made the call.

Carl walked forward and said to a group of people, "This guy pulled a gun on me. Do you guys know him?"

A few people shrugged and one guy said, "He's the dude that was arrested for those roofie rapes a couple months ago. He was out on bail."

Miss Hard Body said, "No shit? That creep was eye fucking me all night."

Carl was constantly amazed at this new generations' casual use of profane slang. "Do one of you have some water I could have? I have cancer and I've been a little sick."

One of the young guys said, "Come on inside where its warmer and I'll get you some water. That dude ain't going anywhere."

Carl stepped inside and sat down on a workout bench. As the young guy went to retrieve a water bottle for him, Carl stripped off his gloves and threw them into a pile of someone's workout cloths.

Six minutes after the shooting call was made the police department responded code three. The responding patrolman didn't know Carl, but the detective that came twenty minutes later did.

The Patrol Sergeant who responded to the call five minutes after the patrolman walked into the gym and sat down on a bench press machine just to watch. The patrolman looked over at the Sergeant to see if he wanted anything and Cam just signaled for him to go ahead. Cam listened to all the conversations and didn't interfere. Carl had never really met Cam, so he assumed he was a typical Patrol Sergeant watching over his people.

"Hello Carl, it's been a long time." Homicide Detective Jim Bratcher was a rookie when Carl was a detective working out of the fraud division.

"Hi Jim, it has been a long time." They shook hands. "Sorry to get you out of bed."

"No sweat, I can use the overtime. So why don't you tell me what happened here?"

"Look Jim, I don't want to be a prick, but we both know that in these politically correct times District Attorneys love to nail cops and ex-cops whenever they get a chance. It's good campaign press for their next election. I think I'm going to lawyer up on you guys. No offense intended."

Jim nodded, "I might do the same thing myself, Carl. No offense taken. Where are the guns involved?"

Carl pointed to the patrolman interviewing some of the gym staff. Carl couldn't help but smile because none of the original witnesses were around. The minute the cops were called most of them split. Carl figured that it was either because they were holding steroids or, more likely, they just didn't want to get their evening tied up giving statements that could mean a court appearance later. That worked for him. The less evidence the better.

Jim walked back to Carl after a few minutes and said, "Carl, we need to take a current photo, get some prints and do a residue test on your hand, so you'll need to ride with us."

Carl nodded, "I know the drill. Listen Jim, I have pancreatic cancer and I'm not feeling too well. Can we make this quick?"

"Sure, do you need to make a call?"

"Ya." Jim handed Carl his cell.

Carl made a call then handed the phone back to Jim.

Jim asked, "Did I just hear you talk with Ambrose McCracken?"

"Yep."

"Swell. Okay you can ride with me. Up front, just like you were innocent."

Sarcasm wasn't new, but these young cops had raised it to an art form.

The police processing went quickly out of curtesy to a sick man. When the tech support lady was swabbing Carl's hands for powder residue Carl commented that they probably wouldn't get much of a test because he'd washed up in the gym restroom.

He explained, "I puked all over my hands outside the gym and after I washed up, I used the gym's equipment alcohol wipes to sanitize myself. When you have cancer, you don't want to catch a cold or the flu. That's the end of the road." He failed to mention his gloves that would have absorbed all the gun powder residue. He had no idea where they were, but noticed the pile of clothes was gone when he left the gym. He figured they were probably scooped up and taken home by accident with the other clothing. With any luck someone had already stuffed them in a washing machine.

CHAPTER 32

There were two interesting meetings occurring that next week. One, at Angie's Diner, consisted of the 10-35 club members; and the other, at the PD, consisted of the narc squad. They both had the same goal: they wanted to know what the other group was up to.

George Codoni looked at Carl, "Nothing to eat, Carl?"

"I couldn't keep it down. This hot chocolate is fine."

Tony Spencer said, "You don't look so good, partner. Can the doctors help you at all?"

"They can give me stronger drugs, but that just makes you sleep which robs you of the little time you have left."

George wanted to change the subject, "Well, whatever your condition, you got it done. That's what counts."

Carl shrugged, "It didn't exactly go as planned. I had to improvise and go to plan B, but I think it will hold up. I know they suspect something because Jim Bratcher asked why I just happened to be in the alley at that time of night being such a sick man. I didn't respond to him of course, but it does tell me that he isn't buying the coincidence story. It really doesn't matter. By the time they figure out what happened I'll be a box of ashes someone gets to sprinkle over the edge of a boat."

Everyone was quiet for a few moments then Tony offered, "I had a talk with Ambrose and he tells me that you two have things all worked out."

"Ya, he's talked with the investigators and gotten them to agree to notify him if they want to talk with me and he's already filed papers with the court complaining about the hour I had to spend at the PD being processed the other night. They know he's laying the groundwork to sue them if they arrest a sick old man. He's being a full-blown prick defense attorney. The kind we used to hate when we were working. Now, I love that nasty old son of a bitch." Everybody laughed.

Ambrose McCracken was a famous ball-busting defense attorney who happened to work for Cam's childhood friend Jimmy Scallon. Ambrose helped Cam when he did an off-the-books rescue of Jimmy's niece. He could be difficult and most cops didn't want to cross him because it could get ugly.

George asked, "So where are the holes in your story?"

"I don't see a lot. I was following him based on the rape victims' website information to make sure he wasn't attacking other women. He confronted me in the parking lot and pulled a gun. I shot him. The plastic bag in the gym bag with solvent residue proves he had the gun originally. He had gunpowder residue on his hands from shooting at me twice. Two pieces of spent brass. No prints on the gun, ammo, or internal parts. No witnesses. My word against his, so to speak."

Tony smiled, "They can't charge someone with a hunch. They've got to have evidence."

Carl nodded, "That's how I have it figured and it doesn't have to work for long. A few weeks from now, all I'll be doing is lying in bed. I doubt the government will want to pay for that."

"And by the way, do you guys remember in the movie, The Patriot, how the British officer looked when Mel Gibson stuck him in the gut with the bayonet? Well, I recently saw that look on a guy's face. To describe him as being astonished and shocked, doesn't really do it justice."

∞

Cam opened the meeting with a rundown on Carl's shooting at the gym. All the Sergeants, Corporals and Lieutenant Glen listened as Cam explained the details of the shooting.

When he was finished everyone paused for a moment to digest the information. Jesse looked at the only old timer setting in the meeting and asked, "Throwdown?"

Glen tilted his head to the side and said, "Maybe, but that might not have been the first plan. ID tells me that the gun was completely wiped down inside and out as well as the ammo. There weren't the normal prints you'd find on a gun and of course it comes back registered to a guy who sold it at a gun show four years ago out of state. No record who bought it."

Cam added, "The alley parking lot camera had been shot out a couple of days before. First time that ever happened to the gym. These guys are good. I sat in the gym and listened to the Detective interview Carl and he lawyered up first thing. Then he called our old friend Ambrose."

Glen leaned back in his chair, "Damn! We just hit a dead end." He stroked his chin hairs for a few seconds. "Any ideas?"

Erin answered, "I've been looking into the group of retired guys that Earl Yoki told us meet with Carl and Tony Spencer for breakfast, but I need more time. All my instincts tell me that when something seems too coincidental to be an accident it isn't."

Jesse said, "Someone needs to touch base with ATF and talk with the clerk at the gun store."

Bobby was a little hesitant to admit his ignorance, but his curiosity trumped his instincts. "I think I know what a Throwdown is, but to be clear, I could use an explanation."

Erin added, "Ya, we youngsters have heard the rumors but…..."

All heads turned to the Lieutenant. Glen nodded, "In the good old days, some of the officers used to carry an untraceable second weapon as a backup, especially when autoloaders were new and not as dependable as they are now. The wheel gun lovers would call automatics Jammamatics, so the old timers felt more comfortable knowing they had a second weapon that wouldn't malfunction. They could also throw them down at the crime scene if they shot someone and found that they were unarmed. You could put the gun in the stiff's hand and fire a couple of rounds, so the powder test would come back positive on the dead guy's hand. There was a case in New York where the crook was supposed to have thrown his gun in a river and when the divers looked, they found seven guns. The cop's buddies thought he might need some help." Everyone chuckled. "It was said that when a mob guy threatened a cop and law enforcement believed it was credible, the crook would occasionally die and a cold weapon would be found at the scene wiped clean of prints. The investigation was usually closed as a mob-on-mob hit. When the mob or any organized group of crooks starts using guerilla tactics against the police, its suicide to line up like 16th-century British soldiers and walk down the street. So, that's why it happened back then. We've come a long way."

Erin looked Glen directly in the eyes, "Did you know any of the old timers that we're looking at to carry them?"

Glen smiled, "Okay, you guys work on the few leads we have and keep me informed." He stood and everyone else followed his lead. Bobby looked at Erin and raised his eyebrows. Erin smiled at him thinking, "I don't think Glen liked my last question."

CHAPTER 33

Tamera Kohl was often misunderstood. She came off as nerdy and shy because of her computer tech skills and the fact that she was quiet, but in reality, she was an aggressive and disciplined young woman. She used others' prejudices to her advantage. When they thought she wasn't going to be a competitor, they would soon find themselves destroyed. She was not the kind of person who avoided responsibility. No cheap, self-serving rationalizations danced through her head. When she was responsible for something, she owned it, and she knew where her responsibility was with the death of Amber Campbell.

She never mentioned that she knew Amber when she developed the very detailed website tracking the roofie rapist. To her it was one step in making atonement for her mistake, but that was just the beginning. There were multiple reasons she developed the web site. It would inflict misery on the rapist, provide her with critical tactical information, and create a smoke screen so thick and wide that you could hide a herd of elephants.

Tamera's day began like any other. She would wake up early and do a workout following a CD of some exercise guru, then eat her avocado toast and drink her energy shake. She cleaned up, jumped in her car and had one small errand to run before she went to class.

She drove out to a country road that had slight curves and a wide shoulder that made it a favorite of cyclists. They could pedal for a ten-mile stretch uninterrupted and then connect with two other options for another six-mile ride. Weekdays meant that there were fewer cyclists, but she was sure she'd see who she was looking for. After all, it was on her website.

Tamera parked on a side street on the north end of the road closest to the city limits and watched while she sipped from her water bottle. After ten minutes she thought she saw Bradley Pope pedal by. She dropped the car gear shift into drive and drove out of town past the cyclist. She slowed down in a somewhat obvious way to make sure it was the rapist and, when she was sure, she accelerated away. Bradley should have been suspicious, but he didn't seem to react, she guessed because many people slowed when passing bikes.

Tamera drove down the road about three miles and, not seeing any other cyclists, pulled into a side street. She popped the trunk and hood release on her car and removed two tires from the trunk that where lashed together with some thin nylon cord. Tied onto both of these tires was a 2x4 about a foot long by some more cord, leaving an 18-inch separation. She dropped the 2x4 into the engine compartment and hung the tires over her front left fender. She'd found these tires in her grandfather's orchard. He was always cussing a blue streak because assholes were constantly dumping garbage on his land rather than paying the landfill fee.

Just for extra protection for the fender, she slipped an old dog bed she'd been meaning to throw away under the tires. She slammed the hood shut and, although it was a tight fit, the cord she used was thin and allowed the hood to latch. Her car was an old Honda that had been passed down through the family. It ran pretty well but had scrapes and dings everywhere because the car was twelve years old and its previous driver, her mother, seemed to consistently park by brail.

She pulled back onto the roadway and headed north toward Bradley Pope picking up speed. She knew that hitting someone with a car was in effect murder and that the natural instinct was to hesitate or chicken out. Assessing the logic, Tamera had concluded that the way to get this done was not to over-think it and remember what had happened to Amber Campbell. It was not unlike jumping into cold water: don't think about it or you'll chicken out. She pictured Amber's face and accelerated to 60 mph. As she approached Bradley Pope, she had but seconds too double check the bike and clothing to make sure it was him and verify that there were no other cyclists or cars nearby. She hung two wheels over the white line as she approached and slowed to 55 mph. Everything seemed to shift into slow motion for a moment. Pope looked up at her when he saw her over the white line, but didn't panic because the car appeared to be going straight. At the last second Tamera swerved to the left, impacting the bicycle without braking. The impact didn't make the noise or feel like Tamera thought it would. Everything was dramatically muted, giving it an almost make-believe reality. She was concentrating on keeping control of the car and getting it back into the correct lane, but did see the bike and the rapist flying through the air. She assumed he was dead because no one could survive an unprotected crash like that, but she didn't stop to see. She'd already made up her mind that she'd read about it in the paper with everyone else.

Tamera pulled over on the same side street she'd initially used to watch Pope pedal by. She popped the hood and trunk again and removed the tires and dog bed, placing them in the trunk. She examined the fender and noticed a minor dent and a slight crack in her head light, but the light still worked and, given the condition of the car, the damage would never be noticed. There was a dumpster next to her favorite parking spot at the college, where she planned to unload the tires and dog bed. On her drive to class, she was surprised at her reaction. She didn't feel guilty at all. She hoped it wasn't a sign that she was a sociopath. They'd been studying that in her Psych 101 course, but she knew she was capable of feeling guilt, because she truly felt responsibility for buying Amber booze the night she was raped. There was a reason they put an age limit on buying liquor and she'd fucked up by ignoring it. At least she'd made some amends today. Her grandfather would be proud of her, not that she would ever tell him. He'd been the one to teach her that a secret is only a secret if you don't tell anyone. He'd also made it clear that there's nothing more pathetic than not acting when you have a just cause. She was sure he'd straightened out many injustices over the years because after her father died and she was adopted by her mom's new husband, Thomas Kohl, her grandfather George Codoni was the real male role model in her life. She loved his police stories and he was still her hero.

∞

Bobby couldn't believe it when Terrence called him, "You need to get out here to this hit and run scene. You're not gonna believe it."

Terrence wasn't very forthcoming. He wanted Bobby to drive across the whole city to see an accident scene? It took Bobby 45 minutes at what should have been his getting off time.

"So, Terrence, what's the, 'you're not gonna believe this,' thing I've gotta see?"

Terrence motioned with his hand for Bobby to follow him. They stepped under a crime scene tape that was tied between the door handles of two sheriff's office patrol cars parked forty feet apart on the west side of a rural road.

Terrence said, "Step on the grass, they may try for some tire prints over in that dirt."

Bobby and Terrence stopped at the top of the rain run-off ditch and looked at a dead body and a mangled bicycle.

Terrence led the way down into the bottom of the ditch. "Just stay where I'm walking. This area's been trashed by all the emergency responders who checked to see if he was alive."

After they stopped in front of the body Terrence asked, "Recognize him?"

Bobby said, "He's not looking too good Terrence. I don't think his mother would recognize him."

Terrence shrugged, "It's our rapist, Bradley Pope. Now look at his arm and pant leg."

Bobby bent over for a closer look. "Looks like tire marks, rubber skids or something."

Terrence nodded, "Yep, that's what everybody thinks, but he wasn't run over."

Bobby was confused, "So what's the story?"

"Don't know. Guess we'll have to wait for the autopsy, but one thing's for sure. There won't be a roofie rape trial. Those old boys are three-for-three."

With the help of Captain Johnson, detectives got the county's autopsy of Bradley Pope moved to the front of the line. All three suspects in a county-wide investigation involving over a hundred victims were dead and the public pressure to explain this was intense.

The county pathologists report said, "It appears as though he was hit at a very high speed by a motor vehicle. His injuries are consistent with an auto versus bicyclist scenario. I would estimate the impact speed to be in excess of 50 mph based on the tissue, organ and bone damage. The location of the body in relation to the POI (point of impact) is consistent with that estimate." Pope had been airborne for 35 feet. "Death was a result of ruptured organs and internal bleeding as well as a fractured cervical vertebra. The secondary impact resulting from the ground appears to have broken the victim's neck. The rubber tire marks located on the body's left arm and left trouser leg were a result of tires hitting the victim, but do not match the tire prints taken from the ground at the crime scene. They were impact marks, not the result of a vehicle driving over the body."

The examiner had his ideas about what had happened, but he learned early in his 30-year career not to tell homicide detectives his theories unless he was asked. And he hadn't been asked.

CHAPTER 34

Captain Johnson walked into Captain Jenkins's office. As Jenkins looked up from his desk Johnson said, "Raymond, we need to talk." He shut the door, which caused Jenkins to think he wasn't going to like this conversation.

"Okay, Bob, what about?"

"Our mutual friend Lieutenant Bud Glen has told me quite an interesting story and since you head up Administration, which is over Internal Affairs, I think it might be your problem as well as mine. As the saying goes, misery loves company. Since our friend Glen isn't prone to sharing unless he has to, I'm sure he believes misery loves company also."

"Bud has a way of unearthing the smelliest messes, doesn't he?"

"No argument there."

Captain Johnson scratched his head, "Where to start? It seems that the roofie rape, and several homicides are all tied together. The kicker is, it may involve a few ex-cops from our city."

Jenkins raised his hand in a stop motion. "This sounds like a long story and I've got to pee and get some more coffee. You want a cup?"

"Sure."

When Jenkins returned with two cups of coffee he said, "I know I'm going to regret this, but go ahead with your story."

"So, we've got this group of three rapists that Sergeant Fulham busted using her patrol officers and narcs. That case spawned a victim's rights group and a website. One of the members is a daughter of a retired cop."

"Cam Michaelson starts using his narcs and patrol officers to surveil parolees and in the course of letting a robbery go down that probably should have been stopped, he discovers a group of retired cops who apparently were looking to buy a cold gun. One of the cops is the father of a roofie rape victim."

"Now we have three dead rapists. One commits suicide in the jail. One is the victim of what looks like an intentional hit and run and the third is shot by an ex-cop with a terminal disease."

Jenkins was accustomed to strange stories and low-grade chaos, but this string of events might achieve a new record. "I've heard reports of some of these things, but I missed the linkage. What's your assessment, Bob?"

Captain Johnson sipped his coffee, "Well first of all, it was a huge fucking error to let the narcs nest in two houses. The crossover has stirred up more shit than you can imagine. Arresting council members' family and stepping on everyone's jurisdictional toes. I got a call from the head of Parole yesterday and they're pissed about us not notifying them about our parolee stakeout program. Hell, I didn't even know we had a parolee stakeout program. These crazy assed narcs think the whole world is their playground and they don't much follow any rules. Did you hear the story about that shaved ape Todd Wilms, throwing a suspect off a loading ramp onto another suspect?"

Jenkins laughed, spraying some of his coffee. "Are you serious?"

"That's the story. I didn't ask any questions though, I've got enough to do without stirring up more crap. It's just a matter of time till the Chief hears about this and opens another investigation."

Jenkins said, "Well Bob, there's another way to look at this. These narcs are finding a lot of crime that would otherwise have gone undiscovered. They aren't doing it by the rules, but they're doing it."

"Ya, there's that, but it causes folks like us to play clean up and some of the problems aren't easily cleaned up. My career barely survived that councilman investigation."

Jenkins knew there was something particular that triggered this get together. Johnson didn't share problems freely because he was ambitious and viewed other Captains as competition.

"Is there some particular problem that has you worried, Bob?"

Johnson knew Jenkins to be a cautious and tactical survivor and didn't want to approach this problem from a position of weakness that could jump up and bite him later on; however, he did need some help, so he'd just have to trust him.

"Ya. The retired cops operating outside the law could be a problem. This looks to be a shit storm that'll consume the whole department and everyone who touched it."

Jenkins nodded, "That would be my assessment also. Tell you what, why don't we tell Lieutenant Glen to ascertain his best information and meet with us privately to develop a strategy for dealing with this. And Bob, tell him we're not ready to have any official reports or memos created. This is just a verbal discussion at this point."

Captain Johnson knew exactly what Jenkins had in mind. The question that gets asked in any internal investigation was, "What did you know and when did you know it?"

Johnson stood up, nodded and said, "I'll be in touch, Raymond, and thanks."

∞

Johnson told Lieutenant Glen about his meeting with Jenkins. He expressed his concerns and told him he wanted all the information he could get, ready to go for a meeting with the three of them in a week. He added, "No reports yet, we're still in the planning stage."

Glen too, knew what "No reports," meant. He had one piece of the puzzle yet to complete. He'd need to get Erin and her compatriots working on that.

CHAPTER 35

Jesse and Randy were tickled pink to be working on a case that wasn't dangerous or politically loaded. This coke snorting and sex extorting attorney was just a fun investigation. Kind of a vacation case. It was always a pleasure to screw with a sleazy lawyer and the fact that there were no guns involved was icing on the cake. It also allowed the two cops to be creative. The informant on this dope deal was a prostitute who got caught selling a little coke on the side to support her habit. She got pissed at her attorney because he was doing a shitty job of defending her and was extorting sex and coke for his payment. She decided to take Jesse up on his offer to get a sentence reduction by being an informant. She also sweetened her end of the deal by not only giving up her coke connection, but doing her attorney also. Jesse was so jazzed that he worked out a deal with the DA to get her probation with credit for time served, if it all came down as she said.

Jesse and Randy needed Erin's help because they were dealing with a female and she had to be searched.

"Okay Jesse, what is it you need a female officer for," she asked?

"Randy will go with you, and I will pick up our informant and meet you at the park on 16th street. You'll search her for us, so we can swear in the report that she didn't have any coke on her before we supplied her with our controlled substance. We also need you to help us wire her."

Erin was about to ask Jesse how he was planning to wire a prostitute who was about to trade sex for legal services without getting caught, but didn't get very far.

As she started to talk, Randy, who had the video surveillance all worked out, interrupted her using his best "Sergeant Friday" voice, "Just the facts ma'am. Just the facts."

Erin, who was close to having steam come out her ears, stepped up to Randy, just inches from his face, "Officer Randolph Keen, get your butt out to the car, now!"

Jesse smiled and shook his head at Randy.

Randy sheepishly grabbed some paperwork off his desk and silently stopped beside Erin's desk. He pointed to her guitar case and nodded. Erin nodded and he grabbed her guitar on the way out the door.

Jesse smiled at her irritation with Randy and said, "Be gentle, Oh Irish Warrior." She made a mock pistol with her index finger and thumb pointed at her head.

When the officers met the informant at the park restroom, Erin took her into the handicapped stall and searched her, making sure she was clean. Erin took Keisha's purse and gave her an undercover one provided by Randy. The two men and two women went to a picnic table where the cops explained what was going to happen.

Erin started, "Okay, Keisha, this special cell phone isn't activated yet, but when I punch it up, it will video and audio record the transaction. I'll slide the phone into this inside purse pocket so the camera can view the scene through this mesh covering. You have to be careful to not block it. It shoots a pretty wide-angle picture, but you need to set the purse where it gets a good view."

Keisha was a street-smart woman of about 30 and was actually enjoying this caper. "It will be fun fucking this asshole instead of being fucked by him."

Jesse had told her not to dress too seductively because courts have viewed that as entrapment in the past, so she wore a short black skirt and a dark blue blouse over black underwear, along with high heels. Jesse had told her dark colors worked best for their purposes.

Randy handed her two, small sandwich-sized baggies with a white powder in them, "Keisha, these have a little bit of cocaine in them mixed with procaine. That will make Counselor Duane Jones think he got some good stuff and the real coke will let us charge him, but I wouldn't recommend you try any because I've added a tracking chemical that is sure to make a big mess and upset his digestive system. Capiche?"

She nodded, "Ya, I get it."

Jesse said, "We will be monitoring the camera picture and listening to your conversation. It's important that you make him ask for sex and coke. You can't offer it or its entrapment. Make him beg for it a little, to show it was his idea."

Keisha nodded, "Ya, just like when I'm working the bars. Make the John ask for sex, never mention it first, right?"

Jesse smiled, "Exactly. Randy, did you come up with a bust signal for Keisha?" Jesse looked at her and said, "When you give the signal, we'll know he took the coke and tried to have sex with you. Then we'll bust him. Keisha, you don't need to screw him for us to make a case. It's the coke part of the bust that will nail him."

Keisha shrugged showing her indifference.

Jesse asked Randy, "So Randy what's our bust signal?"

"You screw like a Kangaroo."

Erin frowned, "Why that goofy phrase, Randy?"

"I like it when things rhyme. Don't give me a hard time."

Erin said, "Jesus!"

Jesse stood up to neutralize his two partners and said, "If there are no questions, let's get moving. I've got some ID people and a Special Masters waiting in the wings to help us."

Keisha looked these three cops over with a skeptical frown and thought, "These crazy motherfuckers are nothin like any cops I've ever seen before. I kind of like them, but they could be lunatics."

Erin and Keisha drove behind Randy and Jesse to the law office of Duane Jones and were right on time for her 2:00 pm appointment. As Keisha went in, Erin walked back to Jesse's car so she could monitor the conversation on their receiving phone. Even if the picture wasn't good, they'd still have good audio because that didn't require the proper alignment.

Erin asked, "Okay, guys, what's the added magic stuff in the coke?"

Jesse gestured to Randy, "Ultraviolet theft detection powder. Security organizations put it on property to prove someone touched it. The classic sting is to put it all over a charity donation box, then when someone steals from it, they light up like a Christmas tree under a black light. We figured if the defense attorney claims it was Keisha's we could show he handled it and, if we're lucky, ran some up his nose. That's what the ID guys are for. They've got a black light set-up and camera's that will record the results."

"You two must sit around all day dreaming up this crazy stuff."

Randy looked at Jesse and they both nodded.

Jesse asked the Superior Court judge who signed the search warrant for the office of Duane Jones to assign a Special Masters to help with the search. The courts require a neutral attorney who is a member of the local bar association to search an attorney's files, so that law enforcement didn't get to read legal defenses and other confidential material possessed by lawyers. The Special Masters only takes documents related to the search warrant authorization.

After Keisha walked into the single-story law office, which was really a 1930's home that had been renovated for commercial lease, the officers sat in their undercover unit watching the video feed. Keisha had placed the purse containing the phone camera beside her on a small end table and pushed it back just a little, so it gave a view of her right side and a full-frontal view of Jones's desk. The picture was excellent and the sound even better.

Erin asked, "So, what's the plan on the rescue and arrest?"

Jesse said, "We don't figure there's a huge hurry since Keisha could probably kick this jerk's ass and there's no indication of violence. I thought we'd just go in and arrest him when she gives the bust signal. ID is having coffee with our Special Master on the next block over. We'll call them in when we make entry."

Erin asked Jesse, "How about the sex act?"

Jesse smiled and said, "Sure!"

"Very funny. Is that island humor or did you learn that in charm school?"

Jesse continued, "I don't think she'll be too traumatized by his advances and I told her she didn't need to let him have at her, so that should cover us in court."

Erin nodded, "So we sit back and wait for the bust signal, I guess?"

"Yep."

Keisha worked it like a pro and Duane Jones came on like an actor in a bad porno movie.

"Hey baby, what did you bring me?"

"What do you want?"

"Pussy and blow. Not necessarily in that order."

"How'bout we talk about my case?"

"I got that covered. Now, did you bring me some coke or not?"

That's when Keisha sat the two baggies on his desk. He picked them up like a starving prisoner and opened one of the Ziplocks. Randy had purposefully filled both bags to the point of stressing the bag because he wanted a mess when they were opened. He got his wish. Some of the powder spilled onto the desktop and Jones bent over and sniffed it right from the desk. He used one of his business cards and his free hand to scrape up the remainder and put it back in the baggy. While his head was still buzzing from the rush, he stood up and made his move on Keisha.

He was clumsy and aggressive, pawing her breasts and trying to get his hand up her skirt.

"Come on baby, let's see the good stuff. You don't want your lawyer pissed at you, cause jail really sucks."

He got Keisha's dress pulled up and didn't notice her adjusting her purse on the end table. He pulled down her underwear and dropped his pants.

Just as he was trying to get her turned around to sit on his desk, he heard her say, "I'm not sure I want to do this, you screw like a kangaroo."

Jones wasn't into women saying no. "Oh, you're going to fuck me bitch because your future depends on it."

Jesse, Randy, and Erin were out of the car and moving when they heard the word "Kangaroo." As Jesse entered the office, he badged the secretary and walked right past her to Jones's office door. It was locked.

Erin badged her and said, "We have a search warrant. The key, now!"

The secretary who thought Duane Jones was a disgusting pig handed Erin her loaded key ring and said, "The big, gold-colored one."

Erin announced "Police Officer, Search Warrant," as she opened the door. She stood back as Jesse and Randy went in. They found Keisha sitting on the edge of the desk and Jones sitting in the guest chair facing the desk with his pants and underwear around his ankles. He was holding his throat where Keisha had delivered a short quick punch. Randy grabbed him by his shirt and stood him up so he could cuff his hands behind his back.

Randy had already called the ID techs and the Special Masters when they were on their way into the building, so they arrived a few minutes later.

Jesse told the ID guys, "I want you guys to light everything up and take your pictures before we seize any evidence. I think you're going to find it everywhere." The ID techs told him that the ultraviolet pictures show better in low light, so they shut all the blinds and turned out the lights. The purple smears were everywhere. They snapped pictures of the desktop, Jones's nose and face, his hands, his dick where he grabbed himself and, of course, Keisha's boobs where he mauled her.

As they were snapping pictures Keisha said, "You'll probably want a few pictures of this." She pulled up her skirt bending over slightly and wasn't wearing her underwear because Jones had removed it. She turned around and displayed multiple smeared hand prints on both cheeks of her ass.

The cops started laughing and Randy told Keisha, "Let's see him deny this one."

Jones was transported to jail and the search of his office was executed.

The Special Masters attorney found more evidence of ethical misconduct and forwarded his report and evidence to the court, who eventually would forward it to the bar association as well as the DA's office.

Randy told the ID guys, "I'm going to need copies of all those photos you took here today."

Erin gave him a judgmental look.

"Strictly for professional purposes, Sarge."

CHAPTER 36

Erin thought the Duane Jones coke case was a nice break from reality, but she had some serious work to do. She'd assigned Anna Sims and Bob Volk to do some research for her. Both of them had approached her separately about a transfer to the narc squad, so they were anxious to show their work ethic. She had them try to identify officers who socialized with the group of retired cops that had breakfast every morning at Angie's Diner. She told them to be subtle and that Earl Yoki might be a good place to start. The kicker was she wanted them to go back as far as they could, even if it was ten years.

Then Erin assigned Al and Tommy to research two things. The first: officers from their agency that had died in the last ten years locally. The second: suspicious or accidental deaths of criminals in the area over the last ten years. The three narcs got together and decided that a list of dead crooks was almost infinite because of their violent, drug-laced lifestyle, so Erin told them to limit it to child molesters, rapist and murderers. She figured that other crimes wouldn't be serious enough to trigger these ex-cops.

She had trouble believing that they'd come up with anything that was tangible because this was such a speculative thing, but it never hurt to try.

Al and Tommy asked Erin why she was using her patrol officers for this investigation, feeling a little sidelined.

"I don't know if you guys noticed, but patrol often doesn't completely trust us narcs. I figured that a patrol officer being questioned might be more open with one of their own. Besides, we're really busy right now and those two want to schmooze for a transfer."

Al said, "Right, makes sense."

Anna was able to get one of the older guys to take a trip down memory lane because he knew her uncle who was a cop and it didn't hurt that she was pretty. He started listing all the guys that used to meet for breakfast and had passed away. Bob Volk took a different tack. He got pictures of all the deceased officers from the last several years and did a photo lineup to have the diner employees look at. Between Anna and Bob, they came up with a pretty solid list of participants. The only problem was that the inquiry got back to the 10-35 club.

Al and Tommy's research netted a list of 15 names that fit the criteria, but didn't see how they'd tie any death to any one suspect. They handed Erin all their data and said, "For what it's worth."

Erin talked with Jesse, Cam and Bobby at a staff meeting about her investigation. "How do we cross correlate this information."

Cam looked at Bobby, "Just like the parolee 211 predictions?"

Bobby said, "Ya, I could ask Data to come up with something that would match deaths of suspects with later deaths of cops. It could look for MO factors in how the suspects died."

Jesse, with a worried look on his face, said "This is explosive stuff we're talking about here. We can't let outside help understand the results. I think we need to code the retired officers as suspect A, B, C, etc. and the homicide victims as victim 1, 2, 3, etc. If word leaks out about this, we'll be dead center of a category four political hurricane."

As the four supervisors sat around the table and quietly looked at one another, it began to sink in what an ancient sealed tomb of destruction they were about to crack open.

Bobby and Al loaded up all their investigative information after it was converted to code letters and numbers, then went to visit Data.

Data looked up from his computer display, "So, run this by me once again. "

Al said, "We just want to see any cross correlation between the suspects listed with letters and the victims with numbers. Any consistent factors or predictors."

"Okay, is there a reason you coded these people? Could it be a hot potato or is it that you just don't trust me?"

Bobby put his hand on Data's shoulder. "Maybe we're just trying to protect you, Data."

"Right…. I'll get this back to you in about three days if that's okay."

Al nodded, "That'd be great. Thanks."

When the report came back from Data, Cam called another meeting of the supervisors and asked Lieutenant Glen to attend.

He started, with, "Lieutenant, Erin has been taking the lead on this so I'll let her explain where we are."

"Well, I pulled all the suspect death reports that fit our criteria: perverts, rapists and murderers. Doesn't mean there aren't other possibilities, but they were the most logical targets. Of the fifteen, seven deaths are suspicious as hell and three are possibly suspicious. The other five don't appear to have anything to do with us. Data's cross correlation shows that of those ten possible homicides, nine of them occurred within a five-month window before a cop died from our breakfast club. In four of the deaths there was a direct tie to an investigation that was conducted by one of the breakfast club alumni. I didn't include the last shooting of Brian Defoe or the hit-and-run in this report."

Everyone was silent and all eyes were on Lieutenant Glen. Cam knew about this because Erin had reported to him as the ranking supervisor. Bobby knew because he helped Erin put all the various pieces together and Jesse knew because he was sleeping with Erin.

Glen grimaced, "Who else knows about this besides you four?"

Erin said, "Nobody has the whole picture but us. Al, Tommy, Anna Sims and Bob Volk have pieces."

Glen added, "Who has this report?"

Erin said, "This is the only copy, but I have it saved on my laptop."

Glen nodded, "I'll take this report with me and you make sure that computer report stays private. After I look into a few things, I'll tell you which way this is going to go. Until then, this is not to leak out. Any questions?"

Everyone shook their head affirming they had no questions.

"Good work, people. You guys are amazing."

As Glen stood up, Erin said, "Lieutenant, the breakfast club knows we know. We couldn't get all this information without tipping them off."

Glen nodded and walked back to his office to think. He reflected, "Knowledge is like an explosive device, sometimes it's raw power and sometimes it's just dangerous." Glen had to figure out what to do about this knowledge in the context of ethical behavior for a sworn law enforcement officer. He learned years ago that some decisions are best fermented for a day.

Glen had a nice meal with his girlfriend Carol on her boat. Sometimes they liked to buy Chinese take-out, sip wine and watch the ocean birds and sunset from the boat slip. He had a good night's sleep and, without ever telling her what was happening at work, made his decision.

He told Carol, "You've been a big help. I think I know what to do."

She said, "That's great. I wish I knew what the hell you're talking about, but I'm happy that your happy." She gave him a sarcastic smile. He laughed, kissed her and patted her butt as he left for work.

Glen was told by Captain Johnson to research this situation and get together with him and Captain Jenkins, so that's what he planned to do. The only thing he had to decide was whether to follow their lead or go it alone. He really didn't trust anyone beyond the moment because even the best of people can go sideways on you. He would talk with the two Captains and see what they had in mind.

CHAPTER 37

Cam phoned Lieutenant Glen because it was Glen's day off and Cam needed to talk with him before he met with Ambrose.

Glen was his typical succinct self when he answered the phone. Caller ID identified Cam or Glen wouldn't have answered it.

"Yes?"

"Hi, Lieutenant. I got a call from our friend Ambrose wanting to talk with me about our breakfast club inquires. So, I'm guessing he knows what we suspect and wants to head it off. He's also representing Carl Blake."

Glen said, "Swell. Why you?"

I'm guessing because the old timers were told it was the narc squad asking questions and because Ambrose helped me on a case not too long ago."

Glen remembered the case Cam was talking about. He'd saved two girls from a drug dealer who was also a human trafficker. Cam did an off-the-books rescue that violated about a half-dozen laws and he barely dodged the charges with the help of Bobby and Ambrose. The fact that he'd put a major crook named J-Tra in prison helped his case also. The department found it convenient to let the incident go.

"Well, Cam, I guess you knew you'd have to pay for this someday."

Cam was silent for a moment, assessing how much Glen knew about helping his friend Jimmy Scallon with the rescue of his niece. He had to assume that anybody as smart as Glen probably knew it all.

Cam answered, "Ya, I guess I did."

"Go talk to him, listen and commit to nothing. You're not in control of this. I am. Contact me when you're done. I have to meet with a couple of Captains soon."

Cam answered, "10-4. And, Lieutenant, ATF interviewed our pawn shop gun dealer. They came up dry."

"Okay, thanks."

∞

Ambrose bought Cam a cheap lunch at a sandwich shop and attempted to extract what Cam knew. He got nowhere.

"Can't talk about an ongoing investigation, Ambrose, and I'm not the one handling the Carl Blake case."

"I know that, Cam. I'm not worried about the Blake case. We'll all be kissing that bye-bye in a few weeks. Carl's in hospice care starting next week. My goal is to make sure a big band of zealots isn't harassing some fine retired cops over some fantasy idea of a conspiracy."

Cam tried to deflect Ambrose once again. "I can't help you with any information about that, Ambrose."

Ambrose was not going to be put off so easily. "You know, Cam, you didn't used to be so pious about police conduct as I remember. Perhaps it's the promotion that's affected the way you look at things."

Cam wasn't taking the bait. He smiled at the attorney over the sandwich he was biting into. "Nice try, Ambrose."

"I could remind you that it's normal for officers to use whatever means are available to save people from dangerous predators. I might even be able to compel testimony to that effect."

Cam smirked, "But, that would be a violation of attorney client privilege and you wouldn't do that, would you?"

Ambrose smiled, "No. I guess I wouldn't. These are good men who gave their life to protecting the public. It would be a travesty to see their senior years trashed by zealots."

Cam placed his sandwich down on the wrapper. "Look, I understand your position. I'm not high enough up the food chain to make decisions about agency actions on something like this. I think you already know where my sympathies lie, but I don't have much juice in this power struggle."

Ambrose nodded. "Any help would be appreciated. Did you hear about Kat?" She was the niece of his friend that Cam rescued.

Cam shook his head.

"She's been attending USC and doing well. She's on the rowing team and running track. Her goal is to be an attorney. Says she wants to be a prosecutor to help people. Prosecutor, do you believe that?"

Cam laughed at Ambrose's fake outrage. "She'll probably be branded the black sheep of the family."

Cam met with Glen and briefed him on the meeting he had with Ambrose. "He doesn't know much and was just fishing for information. My guess is he's trying to kill the investigation before it gets legs. But make no mistake, he's a formidable enemy if it goes to trial."

Glen nodded. "Well, I'll talk with the two Captains and see what they have in mind. Till then, rumor control."

Cam gave a mock salute.

CHAPTER 38

Glen sat in Captain Jenkins's office in a padded chair beside Captain Johnson who was to his right. Jenkins sat behind his desk denoting to the others his seniority.

Jenkins started the conversation. "Well, Bud, why don't you update us on what you've found."

Glen stroked his mustache and chin hairs with his open palm. "My narcs deployed several teams to crack out information. The teams identified most of the ex-cops that breakfast at Angie's Diner and have identified the ones that have passed away. They've also retrieved a list of deaths that are suspicious of rapists, molesters and murderers. I have pulled all the files on those cases and personally reviewed the investigations."

Jenkins asked, "And?"

"And, there's nothing that would justify reopening them. I can't see any leads or evidence that wasn't examined. I even reviewed them in light of improved DNA testing. There's no place to start. You'll never get one of those guys to talk. There simply is no leverage you could use to break them."

Johnson set his coffee on a table between he and Glen, "Bud, how contained is this information?"

"Four of my supervisors have the full picture, but they're used to keeping things confidential and I'd stake my career on their integrity."

Jenkins offered, "You might be doing just that."

Glen went on, "Ambrose McCracken is defending the group along with Carl Blake, so he has some knowledge. I'm sure these old cops didn't tell him anything beyond what he needed to know for Carl's case. There are no reports other than this one." Glen held up Erin's report.

Jenkins nodded and sipped his coffee. "Well, Bob, what's your gut tell you?"

Glen had noticed Jenkins using this tactic before. He wanted other people to suggest a course of action first. He'd sometimes steer them the direction he wanted to go, but knew final decisions go down better if they're not forced on people.

Johnson grimaced, "I don't think it's smart to open a case unless you have some chance of making headway. If we start down this road, we will make national news and accomplish nothing but a departmental smear. Lots of people will get hurt and it'll be for nothing. And let's not forget the history on how whistle blowers are treated. I can't think of a single case where someone was thanked for pointing out an agency's flaw. This Chief hates all things narc-related and just might kill the messenger."

Jenkins added, "Your argument might be right. It could be destructive to lay it all out to our bosses and make it their problem when we don't have proof, and in fact the honorable thing may well be to deal with it at our level."

Glen was surprised. He'd hoped this conversation wouldn't be a cover-your-ass exercise. Glen offered, "All of us can retire comfortably right now. I personally prefer to act based on my ethical judgement as opposed to what's safe." Glen then remembered himself, "But, I'm not a Captain."

Jenkins smiled at Glen's fake modesty, "For now, if we decide to do nothing but wait for further evidence of a crime, we'll need to deliver a message to this group that will be heard. We can't let them continue unabated."

Captain Johnson said, "It should be low-key and personal without fingerprints."

Jenkins looked at Glen, "Like a breakfast chat."

Glen looked at them both. "I can handle that. I might even take my junkyard dog to scare them."

The Captains knew he was talking about Cam. His reputation was set in stone. Many people at the department believed he was reckless, aggressive and dangerous. Glen knew differently, but wasn't beyond using it when it suited him.

Jenkins said to both of them, "To be clear, this investigation will remain informally open while we wait for further leads or evidence of wrongdoing."

Both Johnson and Glen nodded and recognized Jenkins's tactic. He hadn't buried it. He just required more evidence before moving forward. It would make a good defense if something leaked. Cops frequently sit on cases waiting for a break. You didn't get to be a Captain in the cutthroat world of law enforcement without having survival skills. Jenkins would be a Chief someday if his health held out.

Jenkins said as he stood up, "Bud, only the three of us know what a valuable service your narcs did the department by discovering this group. Our intervention most likely saved a huge nightmare for the agency down the road. Like most heroes their contribution will remain anonymous."

"Thanks for coming over, guys. I'm happy with the way we're moving forward on this investigation."

Johnson and Glen took their cue and stood up to leave.

Jenkins added, "Bud, why don't you let me review that report and I'll shred it after I'm done." Glen handed him the report, knowing full well it was Jenkins way of limiting possible leaks.

Glen went back to his office and pulled a copy of the report he'd just given Captain Jenkins from his desk drawer. He folded it in half and slid it into his inside jacket pocket, so he could take it home and put it in a file where he kept all types of interesting documents. He spent an hour that evening sipping a beer and writing a detailed report on the afternoon meeting. When he was through, he printed it, placed it in a self-addressed envelope and mailed it to himself. The sealed envelope, when it returned, would have a postmark and would verify that he had taken notes at the time of the conversation. He wouldn't open it when it arrived, but it would be available for court should anyone ever challenge his role as a subordinate in that critical meeting. It's not that he was paranoid. It's just that he had trust issues.

Glen called Cam that evening.

"Sergeant, meet me tomorrow at Angie's Diner, 6:00 am."

Cam answered, "Okay, and the purpose of this is?"

"We're going to scare some old cops straight."

Cam wasn't surprised by this tactic. It told him all he needed to know about where this was headed. You didn't try to scare people if you were still investigating them or planning an arrest. Cam said, "10-4."

CHAPTER 39

As Glen and Cam walked into the diner together, they saw the group of ten old timers in a side conference room. Glen walked in like he owned the place. "Hi boys, got room for two more?"

George Codoni barely hid his shock, "Ah…. sure Bud. Grab a chair."

Glen and Cam both grabbed a chair from an adjacent table and found a seat around the long table. They were sitting across from George Codoni about in the middle of the table.

George had regained his composure in the time it took for people to make a space for Glen and Cam. "For those of you who don't know Bud, this is Lieutenant Bud Glen from the narc squad and I'm assuming by descriptions I've heard that this is Sergeant Cam Michaelson."

Bud nodded that George was correct. Bud knew about half the group and recognized a few more. Three of the guys he'd never worked with because San Jose was a big agency and some of these guys had been retired a long time.

Bud smiled and said, "It's always nice to see so many old cops fucking the pension system out of a few more bucks."

Everyone laughed and Cam told the waitress, "Just two coffees."

Bud said a few hellos to specific cops he knew and inquired about their families and other details he remembered about them. He asked about Carl Blake's health and George told him that he couldn't attend the breakfasts anymore because he was too ill.

As Glen sipped his coffee waiting for the right time to deliver his message Cam waited and watched. This was Glen's show and he wasn't exactly sure why he was invited.

Tony Spencer couldn't stand the subtlety. He'd been put through an emotional meat grinder lately and wasn't patient with government bureaucracies. "What brings you and your Sergeant to our table, Bud? I'm sure you just didn't happen by."

Glen set his coffee down and smiled. "No, Tony, I didn't just happen by. I've come to deliver a message." Everyone became quiet and listened. Many of the 10-35 club realized for the first time that their actions could cause them real problems. Bud cleared his throat. "Gentlemen, the department has taken notice of your group and conducted an investigation examining your actions over the past decade. We are watching you and will do whatever is necessary to see that the law is followed. If that means we have to embarrass the department and arrest everyone here, then that's what we'll do. It would be an almost impossible case to win, but that doesn't mean we won't go for it full-throttle. Sometimes the best deterrent is a bloody battle. The agency doesn't feel we can let this go unaddressed."

George Codoni was a stubborn old man who didn't take threats gracefully. "As I remember it, you weren't always a by-the-book guy, Bud."

"No, George, I wasn't and I'm still not, but you guys have taken it way beyond the grey area. I have new responsibilities now, and I don't just act for myself. I'm responsible for a lot of people and the future of the department. That was then, and this is now. Things change."

"Before I leave, I want you to consider one thing. I'm invoking what I like to call the nuclear option, Cam Michaelson." Cam was jolted by this surprise, but his martial arts training taught him not to show emotions, so he sipped his coffee with a straight face. Glen continued, "No doubt you guys have heard about Cam's aggressive tactics and disregard for going slow. I might decide to enjoy retirement also, so I've enlisted Cam to follow through with my mission. If we get a hint of one act of misconduct from this group, I will unleash him to rip this little club wide open. That's a battle you don't want. It will impact your finances, your families and your legacy." Glen paused for his message to sink in. "It's over gentleman. You had a good run, but it's over."

Glen stood up and Cam followed his lead. Glen dropped a $10 on the table and they walked out. As they walked to the car Cam wondered what the old timers knew about Glen, but he guessed we all change with the times.

Glen looked over at Cam as they were walking, "So, that was fun. Do you think they'll behave?"

Cam shrugged, "I would. It's not worth it for them to push and see if you're bluffing. The price of being wrong is too high."

"Hope you're right. We'll see."

Cam decided his presence at this event entitled him to a question. "I was wondering how high this tactical decision went up the chain of command?"

Glen nodded, "I'm sure you were. Listen, Cam, if you take over my job when I retire, you'll have to maneuver your way through mine fields like this from time to time. There are times to share and times to hold information close. I've learned a lot of this the hard way. My advice to you is to trust no one. My goal during the time I have remaining is to make sure the department has intelligent, ethical people in critical positions. When it's all said and done, that's all that's left. Did you leave the parts of the world you touched a little better than you found them?"

Cam had known Glen for years and never heard him get philosophical like this. He was shocked into silence.

When Glen returned to the PD, he told Erin and the two Corporals to delete all records of the 10-35 club investigation, explaining that the two Captains controlled the sensitive case now and wanted no leaks. Everyone nodded and Erin wiped her laptop of all traces of the investigation. She had already backed up her work as a standard habit on a stick drive and saved it in a very secure location because, well, you never know....

Not Cam. He printed out Erin's original report before he returned it to her and placed a copy in his mother's safety deposit box on which he was a co-signer.

CHAPTER 40

George Codoni liked a glass or two of cabernet when he watched the evening news. These days alcohol was almost a necessity to tolerate the world as viewed on TV.

He hit the mute so he could think without distraction. The law enforcement grapevine had leaked information on the death of Bradley Pope. He'd been hit by a vehicle that, according to the investigative report, appeared to have tires tied over a fender. Fifty years ago, he investigated a similar accident that went unsolved. The likelihood of the suspect in that case repeating the MO was ridiculous. A more likely explanation was a copycat suspect. Very few people knew about that case and the cops who were involved in the investigation had all passed away. No one from the 10-35 club would have done it if they heard George tell the ancient story because the cardinal rule of the club was "no freelancing." That's how people got caught. The only other person he could think of that might have heard him tell his old stories was his granddaughter. His tales of yesteryear bored everyone else in his family, but Tamera always asked, "Tell me another cop story, grandpa." She'd done this since she was seven and still did it to this day.

If she was the person who hit Pope -- and given her involvement in the case it was possible-- he could not allow her to be hurt. He nodded to himself as he sipped his wine. He would tell the 10-35 club that it was over. If they stopped, the police department would walk away. If they didn't, Cam Michaelson and Glen would crack them like an egg and investigate every thread till they drew blood. Either one of those guys were dangerous, but together they were ruthless. He couldn't risk Tamera being identified. She was the one family member he loved with all of his heart.

CHAPTER 41

The narc squad tried to have a social get-together around the holidays and this year they combined it with a baby shower for Cam's wife Jane. She had delivered two health skinny twin girls and they'd never really introduced everyone to his adopted daughter who was two years old. They also celebrated the promotion of three new Sergeants: Bobby, Jesse and Terrence. Terrence would go to patrol, Jesse to detectives, but Glen had convinced the administration to leave Bobby with narcotics since he had really lost two Corporals. He also convinced them that Cam needed Bobby as a buffer. The department had discontinued the policy of sharing narc Sergeants with patrol. The consensus was that it was too disruptive and that oversight of the supervisors was impossible when they were working in two divisions.

As the evening at Cam's house progressed the women passed around the babies and tried on every outfit, they had bought for all three of them. Todd held Cam's toddler by the hand and was introducing her to everyone there.

Terrence said, "Looks like that little girl has found her own personal giant. Kind of a Shrek thing."

Cam's little sister, who lived in Nevada, came to see the new babies and watched as Cam put a hand on each side of his oldest daughter's giggling face and kiss her on the forehead the way her father used to kiss the kids. She teared up because she recognized that life had come full circle.

Some of Glen's friends were trying to get his retirement plans out of him with little success. The only clue they got was his girlfriend Carol shaking her head indicating it wasn't going to happen.

Later in the evening Randy started to tell the story of Todd throwing the tweaker off the loading dock and some of the people who hadn't heard Randy's rendition of the adventure were laughing so hard it was embarrassing. Todd sat there with a laughing baby on his knee holding both her hands, playing bucking horse, and ignoring Randy.

Randy's finishing line was, "I swear to god, the crook looked like the coyote in the roadrunner cartoon. He just hung there in the air with his arm flapping, trying to fly, then boom, he crashed right on top of this other moron holding the gun. To top it all off, Todd dodged a personnel complaint of excessive force because Councilman Santos told the Chief that he personally saw the guy jump."

Jane opened some of the remaining gifts family and friends mailed to them. Cam's old karate instructor sent a package from Japan with a note that said, "It's never too early." The box contained three tiny karate gis, all three with black belts.

Randy walked away from the group to Erin's car and returned with her guitar.

As he handed it to her, he asked, "You ready?" She nodded and he announced, "Listen up, everyone. Erin and I have a little musical number we'd like to do for you."

Everyone quieted down and several groups walked over to see what was happening. Bobby gathered up the other people in the house and told them that they wouldn't want to miss this.

Erin and Randy sat on stools Cam had brought from his kitchen bar and placed on the patio. Erin started to play the guitar to the tune of a 1960's song by Jimmy Dean, called "Big Bad John," as Randy sang.

Big Bad Todd

Every mornin' at the gym you could see him arrive
He stood six-foot-four and weighed two-twenty-five
Kinda broad at the shoulder and narrow at the hip
And everybody knew ya didn't give no lip to big Todd
(Big Todd, Big Todd)
Big bad Todd (Big Todd)

Nobody seemed to know where Todd called home
He just drove around town and patrolled all alone

He didn't say much, kinda quiet and shy
And if you spoke at all, you just said hi to Big Todd

Somebody said he came from a science lab
Where they stripped away fat and every ounce of flab
And he got extra big from an iron pile
Till nothing was left but a frightening smile
(Big Todd, Big Todd)
Big bad Todd (Big Todd)

Then came the day where the trucks all stand
When a dealer lay waiting with a gun in his hand
Cops were yelling and hearts beat fast
And everybody thought that they'd breathed their last, 'cept Todd

Through the noise and the junk of that ambush hell
Walked a giant of a man that the narcs knew well
He grabbed a saggin' tweaker, gave out with a groan
And like a silent elevator, a man rose all alone.
(Big Todd, Big Todd)
Big bad Todd (Big Todd)

And with all of his strength he gave a mighty shove
Then a cop yelled out "there's a human up above!"
And four men stared from a would-be grave
Now there's only one left down there to save, the crook

With smiles and laughs they walked back down
Then came that rumble down under that clown
And farts and gas belched out of that pile
Everybody knew they couldn't stop with a smile
(Big Todd, Big Todd
Big bad Todd (Big Todd)
Now, they never revisited that worthless dock
They just placed a little graffiti on the very top
These few words are written on that wall
On this spot stood a man that saved us all
Big Todd
(Big Todd, Big Todd)
Big bad Todd (Big Todd)
(Big Todd big bad Todd

The party roared and gave Randy and Erin a thunderous standing ovation. They both bowed at the waist and Randy pointed both open hands toward Todd who sat down his toddler on a chair, stood, grabbing the sides of his baggy workout shorts and gave a curtsy fit for the queen mother.

CHAPTER 42

The new work week started a few days after the party. Lieutenant Glen called Cam's office.

"Are Bobby and Erin working today?"

"Yes, Lieutenant."

"Good. Grab them and we'll meet in my office in five."

"Will do."

Everyone found a seat and Glen started the meeting. "Nice get-together." Everyone nodded their agreement. He looked at Erin, "I didn't know you and Randy were so talented."

She smiled and said, "Thanks, it was fun."

Glen said, "Ya, now back at the real world. Cam, I want you to organize some type of quiet surveillance on the breakfast gang of retired cops. After chewing on this thing for a few days, I've arrived at the opinion, it's not over. I hope I'm wrong, but I don't think so. I know some of those boys pretty well and they don't let go that easy. We might have scared a few off, but I'll give you odds some of them will lay low for a while, then come back strong. Old cops can be stubborn and frequently don't take threats well."

As Erin looked at Glen slightly perplexed on how to follow this order, she asked sarcastically. "What did you have in mind? Following the terminal ones?"

Bobby and Cam winced.

Glen smiled, "If that's what it takes. And Erin, while I'm thinking about it, tell our new Detective Sergeant, Mr. Hale to keep his ear to the ground. Detectives are likely to hear about any suspicious homicides before we do." Glen knew that Jesse and Erin were living together now and was sure they'd have pillow talk about this case.

Erin wondered if Jesse's transfer to detectives was part of a plan to control this time bomb, masterminded by Glen and the two Captains.

While she was thinking about asking that very question Glen terminated the meeting.

"This 10-35 club is your top priority. Dismissed."

THE END

www.ingramcontent.com/pod-product-compliance
Lightning Source LLC
Chambersburg PA
CBHW031955170626
46807CB00006B/2489